BEAUTIFUL
IMAGE

MARCEL AYMÉ

BEAUTIFUL IMAGE

Translated from the French by
Sophie Lewis

PUSHKIN PRESS
LONDON

With thanks to Jonathan Newhouse

English translation © Sophie Lewis 2008

First published in French as
La Belle Image 1941
© Flammarion

This edition first published in 2008 by

Pushkin Press
12 Chester Terrace
London NW1 4ND

ISBN 978 1 901285 67 3

Cover: *Jean Marais* Valentine Hugo circa 1940
Private Collection

Frontispiece: Marcel Aymé
© Rex Features Roger-Viollet

Set in 10 on 12 Baskerville
and printed in UK by TJ International, Padstow, Cornwall

This book is supported by the French Ministry of Foreign Affairs, as part
of the Burgess Programme run by the Cultural Department of the French
Embassy in London.

Ouvrage publié avec le concours du
Ministère Français chargé de la culture—Centre national du Livre

BEAUTIFUL
IMAGE

I

THE DEPARTMENT WAS OPEN to the public between two and four, in a narrow mezzanine office that looked out over a deep, gloomy courtyard. I headed at random for one of the booths, the middle one, and asked its occupant a question. She didn't respond at first, but finished working out a sum and then began another. Losing patience, I repeated my question, not without grumbling at the staff's lack of zeal in providing information to the public. The clerk, a small woman with greying hair and a timorous expression, worked her way methodically to the end of her calculation, then replied in a neutral voice, without hostility:

"You're in the right place. Have you all the documents?"

I handed her a bundle of papers which she examined, neither rushing nor lingering over them, then filed away, leaving the stamped application to one side. Since the wait promised to be a long one, I started to look around this place that I had come to for the first time. On the side that was open to the public, the space was very limited; there could never be much movement here. For the moment I was almost alone, with only an old gentleman wearing a medal, a retired civil servant most likely, for company. On the other side of the row of booths, the office stretched back into darkness, and although it was scarcely two-thirty, one struggled to pick out the furthest tables, which were also the ones with the least light. It's in this shadowy zone that the first lamps clicked on, their green shades casting discrete circles of light within which the clerks' disembodied hands went about their business. Gathering ground little by little, the lights soon reached as far as the row of booths. Finally, on our side, two bulbs lit up in the ceiling and I noted that they too cast a rather paltry light. A few feet away from me, the retired civil servant leant on his silver-topped cane and exchanged pleasantries with the clerk in the neighbouring booth. I learnt that his name was M Caracalla. No doubt he often had business in this office and he was quite proud of it; I saw it in the scornful way he looked at me and in his affected habit of laughing very loudly, the better to show how at home he was here. I almost envied him his ease in the company of his clerk. Mine, hunched over a register, her pen racing, hardly seemed disposed to start up a conversation, although in truth her face expressed nothing more than perfect indifference.

Weary of examining the place and its people, I returned to certain preoccupations that I had put aside on entering this office: a suspended business deal that I was trying to get back on track; my wife's fit of ill humour the day before; a conversation with a tutor that very morning about my son, who was not taking to his Latin. Women's tempers, classical culture, the price of metals ... I felt for a second all these petty worries begin to mingle in my head and to spin round and round with a sickening slowness. Something inside me seemed to come to a halt—and my mind paused too, uneasy—and then started up again almost straight away. I found myself thinking of something else entirely when at last I heard a murmur from behind the window.

My clerk was asking me:

"Have you brought the photographs?"

"Certainly," I said. "Two of them, isn't it?"

From my wallet I took a dozen passport-sized photos and handed two over to the clerk. She laid them on her register without looking at them, reached from her seat for the glue, but before sticking them on glanced over them briefly. I was surprised to see that her eyes lingered on them as if something unusual caught her attention. This sudden curiosity completely replaced her earlier indifference and machine-like manner and I began to think that, having inflicted on me a kind of trial, she was now preparing the way for an intimate discussion to match the one already taking place at the neighbouring window. But, raising her eyes to look at me, lowering them again and raising them once more, she said with a certain animation:

"This is not your photograph."

Dumbfounded, I imagined for a moment that I'd made a mistake, but then I had no trouble recognising the photographs, upside down as they were. The clerk's comment appeared to be a joke. I believed I was meant to laugh.

"Do you think," I said, "that the photographer's art has flattered me so much?"

The clerk didn't even smile. She had let go of her pot of glue and, pursing her lips, was comparing my face with the images in front of her. At last, apparently sure of her facts, she gestured as if rejecting my two photos and said severely:

"Find me some others. I cannot accept photographs which are not of the party concerned."

I refused to take them and protested vigorously that the joke had gone too far.

"All the more since these photos are perfectly good likenesses. I do not see why you should have more difficulties in recognising them than my family, who have seen them and found them perfectly satisfactory."

Still holding the photographs, she was momentarily perplexed. I had a sudden thought that this woman was not in full possession of her reason. Then I began to imagine some bizarre disability which distorted her visual perception, and curiosity postponed my anger for a moment. Finally, turning her head away, she called towards a particular spot in the half-darkness behind her:

"Monsieur Boussenac! I beg your pardon, but would you mind coming over here for a minute, please?"

The deference in her tone implied that she was requesting the arbitration of a superior. Satisfied by the turn the incident was taking, I smiled with benevolent scepticism. Meanwhile, in the depths of the office, between two circles of light, a vague figure gradually emerged from the greenish shadow. M Boussenac was a short podgy man with lively, intelligent eyes and a jovial countenance. His appearance would have reassured me if I'd had the slightest anxiety about the outcome of this business. The clerk stood up, so he could take her chair.

On sitting down, he enquired in a cordial voice to which a light country accent added extra cheeriness:

"Now Madame Passavent, is something wrong?"

"You shall be the judge," replied Mme Passavent with some energy. "The gentleman came to the window to apply for his B O B permit. He provided all the necessary documents, but then he gives me photographs which aren't of him."

"Of course, this is Madame's opinion," I added, with an air of nonchalance that I intended to be insolent. "It is not my own."

M Boussenac gestured politely for me to be silent and began to look through my file.

"Let us see: Application ... I the undersigned Raoul Cérusier, commercial broker, born in ... on the ... 1900 ... residing in Paris, Rue ... good ... birth certificate ... certificate of livelihood ... character reference ... certified in due form ... everything is there. Let us now have a look at the photographs. Where are they?"

Mme Passavent laid them in front of him. After examining me with a penetrating glance, he looked at them and I saw him smile. At the next window, the clerk and M Caracalla had broken off their conversation and were gazing curiously at us, with the prurient hope that the slightest unexpected event always rouses in the hearts of the idle. M Boussenac did not spend long on the photos.

"There has been a misunderstanding," he said. "Monsieur Cérusier has simply mixed up his photographs. He will have no trouble at all seeing this when he has taken the time to examine them himself."

Evidently, M Boussenac was taking Mme Passavent's side. In spite of what for me was plain evidence, I wanted to believe that I had made a mistake. I seemed to recognise, from my side of the window, my two passport photos, but the fact that I was seeing them upside down might be misleading me as to their likeness. M Boussenac handed them to me with an affable smile. At first glance, my certainty was absolute.

"These are certainly my photos," I said, "and I even think I have never had any that so resembled me as these."

M Boussenac became grave and replied in a tone from which the cheeriness had vanished, though it was still conciliatory.

"Sir, believe me, if it were a case simply of a questionable likeness, we would not bother to be so exacting. As far as possible, everyone here strives to facilitate the requirements of the public. But with all the will in the world, we cannot accept these two photographs. That would simply expose you to further annoyances. Not only do they not resemble you, but it is plain that they show a man whose physiognomy is completely different from your own. Look, it's as if I were trying to pass myself off as Mme Passavent."

I had no idea how to react to the absurdity of the situation; all the approaches I could have taken being ultimately ridiculous. I was no longer angry, but an unfamiliar panic stirred inside me. It was within me, in my flesh, a kind of warning which made no sense to me until the second when I thought to myself: "And if he's right? If they no longer *do* look like me?" And this notion, which should have appeared crazy, troubled me to the point that I began to stammer.

"This is harassment," I said. "You're trying to harass me."

At the same time, I looked up at M Boussenac and must have appeared distraught, for he was touched.

"Come," he said softly, "don't persist. There's no shame in recognising that you have made a mistake."

"I give you my word that these are photographs of me," I replied impetuously. "It's incomprehensible. You have seen them wrong. You must have seen them wrong."

"Calm down," the good man persevered. "I don't doubt your intention. It sometimes happens that in a moment of fatigue or annoyance an error sticks in our heads despite the evidence. We are all occasionally subject to this kind of delusion and it's never very serious. We just have to take some time for the truth to become obvious, to gather the evidence. Since my word and that of Mme Passavent aren't enough for you, would you like me to call some others?"

"Please," I murmured.

He called to the two clerks in neighbouring booths. The man with the silver cane came up beside me along with his clerk, even jostling me slightly as he craned to look. The newcomers each looked over M Boussenac's shoulder while he outlined the situation in a few words. I felt their eyes on me and almost instantly, I heard the sentence that each one pronounced as they looked. Neither one clerk nor the other recognised me in the image that they saw. There is nothing in common, they confirmed, between the two faces. Not a single feature.

"You see," said M Boussenac gently.

I was silent. I believe I rubbed my forehead several times, as people do in films or books when they think they're dreaming and can't accept the reality. Suddenly, right beside me, a voice rang out like a furious trumpet. It was M Caracalla, the silver-cane man, who had just been studying the photo left lying in the booth.

"Are you serious, my boy? You have the nerve to claim that *that's* your photo? Well, you're lucky to be dealing with some patient people. If I were in their place, I'd sort you out. You look like a fine scoundrel to me, my boy!"

Instinctively I made some threatening or defensive movement, which prompted the fellow to draw back to his booth, from which he continued to watch me, uttering unintelligible exclamations in a furious undertone. In truth, the spectacle I presented deserved his attention. Without quite realising it, I had taken a step in his direction and I found myself right in front of the glass partition between the booths that separated the public half of the room from that of the staff. A reflection passing over this glass made me turn to look at my own image, but with the state of the lights, the glass was remarkably transparent and hardly reflected anything. Without worrying about disturbing my onlookers, I contorted myself in the attempt to find some favourable angle, bending and stretching, standing back and peering closely—I ended up glimpsing the outline of a head and a few indistinct facial features. In these fragments of lines and shape, I recognised nothing of myself. Then a clerk got behind the window and, by covering one of the lamps, managed to modify the lighting slightly. For a fraction of a second, I had in front of me the reflection of my own two eyes. The image, faint but distinct, was that of two large pale eyes, with a gentle, dreamy expression, completely different from my eyes, which are small, black and deep-set.

The eyes disappeared from the glass but I remained staring, hands on my knees, my mind blank, scarcely forming thoughts—which could only add to my disarray. When I stood up again, M Boussenac and the three clerks were gazing at me with expressions of sorrow and pity, while M Caracalla sniggered, shaking his head. Returning to the booth, I reclaimed my documents.

"We will go through with your application, but it seems to me there is no hurry," responded M Boussenac, with a cautious solicitude that stung me. "You could leave your papers with us and come back another day, or even wait here a moment, just the time it would take to call your home or your office and ask for other photos, couldn't you? Come and sit down over here, then."

He obviously took me for a lunatic and wanted to buy some time in which to alert my family and maybe even the police. Fear gave me the strength to compose a calmer expression and to reply in a voice that was almost serene.

"You are very kind, but I have a meeting that prevents me from waiting. Please excuse me," I added, smiling, "my actions must have seemed very strange to you, but

I've only just begun to understand what has happened. One of my relatives is playing a trick on me, and must have arranged to switch the photos round today. I admit they have succeeded beyond their expectations."

If you gave it any thought this explanation would look quite flimsy, but my tone of voice seemed to reassure M Boussenac. He gave me my papers and we exchanged a few more friendly words. As I headed towards the door, someone grasped my arm and I struggled to suppress an instinctive movement of terror. It was only M Caracalla. He stood there in my path and, gazing at me with an insulting air of compassion, proffered with the sugary voice of a geriatric nurse:

"There's nothing the matter really, is there? You'll be nice and reasonable and let me walk with you to your house. Nice and reasonable, hmm?"

I could see hatred shining in his eyes and was naturally surprised, for at no point had my behaviour justified such a reaction. I have seen the same hatred, similarly tinged with envy like this, in the eyes of old men looking at young people. But I wasn't a young man.

"Thank you," I said, "but I live in the suburbs. I would not want to make you return home late and risk being scolded by your housekeeper."

My reply, which drew discreet laughter from M Boussenac and his staff, enraged M Caracalla. He pulled a face of disgust, and as I reached the door, I heard him spit out behind me:

"You'll pay for that."

II

ON LEAVING M BOUSSENAC'S OFFICE, I set off intending to reach the Rue du Quatre Septembre on foot, with a stop halfway to see a client at about three o'clock to look over an advertising contract with him. I thought vaguely about ways of securing the deal. It seemed as if life was once more taking its familiar path. Although I could not entirely forget the incident with the photos, I was not disturbed by it in the least. I may have felt a slight, as it were, unconscious anxiety. To the memory of my misadventure, I naturally countered the plain impossibility that such a thing could ever happen. In this way I took shelter behind the picket fences of reality—and without much curiosity, for I had a very simple means of testing their worth and was not above resorting to it. This was to stop outside a shop window and look at myself in a mirror. Yet I avoided glancing at the side with all the shops and concentrated on walking right on the edge of the pavement. From time to time, the image of those two big, bright, reflected eyes rose before me. My heart would briefly freeze up with fear, but instantly I put that apparition down to a minor hallucination, and casually noted that perhaps I ought to see a doctor. I even came to recall with amused irony the agonies I had just been through. I was already picturing myself recounting the incident to my wife or a friend. I would tell them: "Something very strange just happened to me; I simply can't explain it." These words, which I repeated to myself with pleasure, had something really amusing about them. I remembered having heard the line many times, pronounced exactly that way. Anybody, I assured myself, could dig up "something very strange which he cannot explain" from the depths of his memory. There's nothing more ordinary. At the time of the experience, it was bizarre, even frightening, but retold, it becomes nothing at all. In reality, nothing had actually happened.

The end of this month of September, so warm and luminous, was like a return to summer. A holiday feeling infused the air of the city's streets and I inhaled it with delight. Increasingly, my misadventure seemed like an episode from another season. Walking down the Rue du Bac, my way was suddenly obstructed by a small crowd gathered on the pavement around a taxi. A dispute over payment had arisen between the driver and his client.

"You must have learnt to read at the Quinze-Vingts eye hospital!" said the driver gesturing towards the cab's meter. "Don't you see that it says fourteen francs?"

The client, a small, elderly man with whiskers and a beige bowler hat, retorted in a rather girlish voice:

"Cabbie, do what you like. Your meter will always be less reliable for me than my long experience as a Parisian. Here then are ten francs and that, I believe, is generous payment."

Straight away the tone of the exchange grew louder, for the driver took offence at the term cabbie. From the far side of the circle of onlookers, I saw that an elegant young lady with a sweet face was watching me with quite a tender interest, and not surreptitiously but with intent, or perhaps more as if she were enchanted. Here I must say that I am not used to finding myself the object of female attention and that, nature having endowed me from the cradle with unprepossessing features, it's only through my imposing presence that I can hope to pique their curiosity. Besides, I love my wife, place a high value on my duties as a father and spouse, and have almost always resisted the temptation of adventures. All in all, I risk very little in the chances of an encounter. I can even take pride in victories won over myself on riskier occasions. This doesn't mean I am indifferent to women—on the contrary—and often the regret of pleasures denied lasts long in my heart and in my flesh, so sharp that I never feel myself so weak, so vulnerable, as when I have just conquered my weakness. It was precisely this kind of regret that I felt on losing sight of the beautiful unknown woman and whilst going on my way towards the banks of the Seine. Her gaze, like that of a delicate animal suddenly discovered, had penetrated mine and touched my heart, and I imagined with a real distress what might have followed. I had forgotten the incident of the photos. Still enervated by my regret, I crossed the river slowly, taking the time to appreciate its views and autumnal banks.

At the end of the bridge I had to wait at a crossing to allow a long line of cars to pass. Next to me a bus was also waiting in traffic and I saw that two very pretty passengers sitting one behind the other were observing me through the window, the one dreamily, the other with a distinctly greedy eye. I should have been surprised but, caught up in the pleasure of pleasing, I thought only that there were indeed some women capable of understanding me at their first glance. As I was modestly looking away, I saw my friend Julien Gauthier standing next to me on the kerb, also waiting to cross. Since the age of twenty-five—when, before committing ourselves to other things, we used to work side by side in our lawyer's practice—our meetings have been irregular, but we are always pleased to see each other. His eyes fixed on the sea of cars, Gauthier might have been dreaming about some new job, since he had given up law roughly a year before I did and had embraced successively the careers of football player, bookseller, couturier and director of a cabaret. At the moment he was an impresario. With a clap on the shoulder, I distracted Julien from his contemplation and said affectionately:

"Hello old man, how are you?"

Gauthier turned round and his face, already dawning with a cordial light, closed up straight away, disconcerted. After looking me up and down for a second, he made a polite smile, as if scarcely amused, and said coldly:

"You must be mistaken."

Julien Gauthier is a serious fellow, as little inclined as could be to making jokes. Quite evidently, he did not recognise me. At this blow, the fear which had gripped me in M Boussenac's office took hold once more. It was a panic, a landslide which swept away all my defences, down to the smallest doubt to which I might cling. I began to tremble, and my face must have been frightening because Julien started speaking softly to me. I stared at him, not hearing his words, watching the world falter in his eyes, which no longer knew me. Taking my horror for madness, he patted my shoulder in an amicable way, though also with a certain persuasive firmness that was terrible to me, for it communicated his wish to hand me over to an officer or a police station. I detached myself with a violent movement, saying in a low voice husky with fear:

"No Julien, let me go. I beg you, Julien."

Leaving him to his stupefaction, I threw myself between the cars, ignoring the drivers' invective and the traffic officer's whistle. Still running, I crossed the Jardin des Tuileries and only stopped when I came to the arcades on the Rue des Pyramides, in front of a shop selling ivory objects. Before looking at myself in one of the mirrors that framed the shop window, I strove to restore order, if not to my spirit at least in my face, which I felt was twisted with fear. My curiosity helping to calm me, I managed to regain the appearance of tranquillity.

On seeing myself in the mirror, I could not resist glancing behind me to make sure that this reflection was not that of a stranger. But when I opened my mouth, wrinkled my nose, knit my brows, the strange face also opened its mouth, wrinkled its nose, knit its brows. Standing on the doorstep, the shop owner and a young assistant were laughing at my grimaces, and their amused curiosity put me to flight. The opinion they must have formed of my conduct was surely so bizarre that I thought seriously about going back to provide them with some plausible explanation. For the first time, I felt that mixture of fear and humility which the consciousness of their exceptional condition, being beyond the appreciation of reason, must inspire in some types of madmen, and which makes them wish above all to pass for normal human beings.

Fleeing the gaze of the two people who could have testified to the strangeness of my behaviour, I turned into the Rue Saint-Honoré, and from then on I understood that I would henceforth devote all my efforts, all my activity, to hiding myself behind the appearance of a normal life. Until my death I would carry the burden of an unspeakable truth, I would suffer silently, a rare pariah in whom the simplest and most fundamental of natural laws had wrought a secret rupture. Nature had chosen me as both witness and instrument of a monstrous deviation, and the necessity of living made me also her accomplice. I felt all the perils that this partial metamorphosis would expose me to, and the instinct for self-preservation was already forcing me to work out how to complete my transformation. I should try not to live in two registers at once, that is, not to show the presence of two people in me, since their discord, if it were visible, could easily have me carried off to the padded cells. My voice, which had not changed, my handwriting, my habits, my feelings towards people, certain ways of thinking and reacting were now traps to avoid. As much as possible, I had to fashion myself a personality that would suit my new face.

I was engaged in these reflections in the back room of a little café close to the Saint-Roch church. After serving me, the waiter left me alone and I could examine myself in the mirror at leisure. There was not a single feature in my new face that recalled the old one. I took out one of the passport photos in order to judge my transformation more precisely. I had to concede that I had gained much in the way of youth and charm. I saw myself now as a man of thirty at the most, with a fine-boned, graceful face, a noble profile, contours at once firm and sleek such as belong to well-nourished, elegant people, and which usually make a great impression on the ladies. My eyes, which were a very light grey-blue, shone with a charming gentleness, and my hair, formerly black, had turned chestnut and was also, it seemed to me, thicker and glossier. Nothing remained of my own face, not even an expression, and this was not the least of my shocks. An expression is after all nothing but the reflection of a state of mind which the face can only interpret.

I was kneeling on the leather seat, my photo in one hand and my nose pressed against the mirror, every so often rubbing away the mist left there by my breath. Even while imagining the extent of my misfortune, I found some comfort in the thought that instead of being improved, I could have been afflicted with repulsive features or even with an ass's head, as happens in *A Midsummer Night's Dream*. I began to think of my old face with a sympathy that verged on pity. That large flattened countenance in the photograph, that jaw and that bulldog nose, furrowed, scowling, those little black deep-set eyes with their sharp, suspicious gaze—I had never considered them with such freedom. I looked at this portrait, which was no longer my own, with the detachment of distance, as if it represented an absent friend, and my personality, my approach to life, appeared to me now as a complete picture, and not an entirely flattering one. I saw or thought I saw in their real light that constant desire for parity with others that sometimes made me mean and unjust, my fear of being taken in, which showed in a kind of aggressive self-importance, a vain desire to feel my authority over those around me, a certain overzealous subservience to money, to power, to the idea that conditions of inequality are what makes the world go round, but also a robust sense of duty and honesty considered as an investment, a loyal dedication to my loved ones, a real generosity which would have been more effective had it not been tempered by an overdeveloped sense of mistrust. These faults and qualities, formerly written on my face, seemed still to be active in me but were already different, having lost some of that congruence and solidarity that had fused them together and made of this combination a distinct individual. It was as if a guiding element had suddenly gone missing. It seems to me that the face is not only a mirror reflecting our thoughts and feelings but that it actually interacts with them and is composed by them. Everyone knows, for example, what the character of a woman may owe to the idea she has of her own beauty. We constantly live with a particular vision of ourselves. For me, when a question of conscience makes me hesitate, my face looks to me like a severe examiner, and I don't make any decision before I've accounted for it, or rather before I've assured myself that this look 'suits' the decision—almost as if I were trying on a hat. At least, that's what I used to do.

I was focusing on these problems of visual correspondence as if nothing could be more important to me now.

But it was a cover, an angle that allowed me to proceed by small steps, only gradually penetrating my misfortune and sidestepping its most painful aspects. More than anything I resolutely avoided the thought of my wife and children. I would have liked, so as to escape the thought entirely, to give myself up to a religious horror of the absurd, but I had only a very human fear, that of an immediate future whose promise chilled me to the core. I ended up sitting down once more with my back to the mirror, trying once again to pretend that nothing had happened and in spite of my efforts asking myself one key question: this evening, in a few hours' time, I should be coming home from work, kissing my wife, my daughter, my son. What am I going to do? Explain to my wife that I have a new face? Unthinkable. She would have to be mad to accept such a tale. To be honest, her credulity would have been less surprising than my metamorphosis, but that thought didn't occur to me then. In truth, I was struck by the accidental nature of the absurd. Having provided reality with a new beginning, with new reference points, this sense of the absurd would discreetly fade away. This groundless conviction was yet another product of my beleaguered reason, which nevertheless had just been obliged to admit an impossibility.

I left at quarter-past three having got nowhere in all this. It was not too late for my three o'clock meeting, but how to explain myself to a client who already knew me? I headed mechanically towards the Rue du Quatre-Septembre and my office. Somewhere on the way, I realised that my transformation now dispossessed me of the business which I had founded and on which I depended for my livelihood. It only existed through me, through the trust, the credit that certain people and places allowed me. A sales broker to start with, the fortunes of my profession had one day put me in contact with some metal importers and I had thus been able to add to my original business an office dealing in tin and lead, which soon took up most of my time. The establishment of this new office had given me some trouble and, while pleased with its early success, I was hoping for better in the near future. Suddenly, all this was over.

Now my office building was within sight, but what was I to do? My secretary would receive me like a stranger. I walked past the doorway, throwing a brief glance sideways, and going on towards the Stock Exchange. My new face was standing between myself and my life like a blank wall. I knew it already, but the test of this very familiar reality made the plain truth more tangible, more aggressive, and threw me into a fit of fury. I rebelled, refusing to abandon everything and allow myself to be walled up alive. No prison exists that cannot be escaped and I was ready to risk anything. I needed to fight, even without a reason to hope.

It was as if my sudden anger had cleared my mind. Certainly my situation remained the same, but I could see a few possibilities for my discreet survival as myself; ways of keeping my own name and that of my company for a while without people being suspicious of me. I turned back the way I had come, determined to enter my own office.

III

A S I RISE SLOWLY TOWARDS the third floor in the old hydraulic lift, I have time to refine certain elements of the somewhat risky plan I've just put together. I stop for a moment on the third-floor landing, straining to hear, heart pumping. I can hear nothing. My office consists of a vestibule furnished as a waiting room and two further rooms, with a small annexe leading to the larger of them. Strictly speaking, this room, which is also the better furnished, is actually my office. In the other room are my secretary and a typist whose desk faces a window opening onto the vestibule, opposite the main door. It is impossible for me to enter without being seen by Mme Lagorge, the typist, but nevertheless I may hope to escape her vigilance. What I fear most is to find a visitor in the vestibule, someone who knows me, or even one of the building's staff on their way to the toilets. Then I would just have to take myself off again, having enquired after M Cérusier.

As I open the door, I pull my handkerchief roughly from my pocket so as to make several coins jump out with it and roll onto the floor in front of me. I've no time to see Mme Lagorge's face; already I am on all fours in the vestibule in pursuit of my scattered coins, and emitting furious exclamations. Mme Lagorge, who can have caught no more than a three-quarter view of my face, recognises me by my voice, my build and my clothes, for she utters little cries of solicitude. There is no one else in the vestibule and, having crossed it on hands and knees, I make it to my office door, my back still turned to the typist's window. This first success encourages me, but I am a little worried not to have heard the voice of my secretary echo Mme Lagorge. Perhaps Lucienne is in my office, where in my absence her work quite often takes her?

Indeed, just as she was leaving for her lunch at midday, I had requested that Lucienne make up a file for which most of the documents were to be found in my drawers. Guarding against all possible glimpses, I pull my hat down over my eyes, though since it's a 'rolled brim' type, it doesn't hide much. For greater safety, I bury my face in my opened-out handkerchief and walk into the office pretending to blow my nose. With this wealth of pre-cautions I manage to stop myself from seeing anything either. I ask mildly: "Any news?" No answer. So I'm alone. I go straight to the cupboard where I keep papers relating to certain unfinished deals, and I open up both cupboard doors so that they form a small corner of shadow where I will shortly find refuge. Then I sit at my desk to write a cheque. I expect Lucienne's knock from one moment to the next. I make haste to accomplish my tasks with the greatest economy of movement. I haven't time to check the state of my bank account, but I know I have about fifty thousand francs. I make out a cheque for forty thousand in Lucienne's name, since they know her there. The cashier won't make a fuss about paying her. I'm still writing the name of the beneficiary when I hear a knock on the communicating door between the two rooms. I say nothing until the second knock, then, leaving the signed cheque on the desk, I run to the cupboard. With my face thrust deep in the darkness of the cupboard it is impossible to see anything of me other than my back and yet I still don't feel completely safe from Lucienne. We have been working together for more than five years and at the end of last year she was my mistress. Our affair only lasted a fortnight, for I found the notion of cheating on my wife unbearable. The fear of being found out and a genuine sense of remorse meant that I lived those two weeks in a sick delirium. Lucienne understood my reasons for ending it perfectly, and told me that she had been expecting as much from the first day. I cannot say I am ashamed of my behaviour towards her. This lovely tall girl of twenty-five had accepted with a reassuring serenity the premature end of the first amorous affair of her life. It is true that since then she likes to take revenge in strange ways, and this often leaves me nervous and humiliated. For instance, when we're working at my desk facing each other, she might calmly lay down her pen or document, take my face in her large, hot hands and gaze ardently into my eyes while, silently, she blushes all over, like a man. Overwhelmed, holding my breath, I await her orders. I even hope for them. She knows it, but if I risk making the least gesture, she drops me with a kind smile and returns to her work. I always feel a terrible disappointment, which fades as soon as I'm alone, and even becomes a point of satisfaction when I have my wife beside me.

Lucienne comes in and straight away I begin to speak, measuring my speech carefully for I fear her shrewdness.

I must, without losing the grave and superior tone which marks my everyday speech, allow a certain discreet buoyancy to enter my voice and words.

"Lucienne, I shall shortly be leaving for Bucharest. I just met that small gentleman Meyerhold from the BBS, who introduced me to Brown at the Metal Union. We had a long conversation about certain possibilities which the Balkan market seems to be offering at the moment; moreover we were already thinking of working together on it."

I invent a story which will make plausible a journey abroad of two or three weeks.

"From Bucharest, I will probably go on to Yugoslavia. But I'll explain everything to you in a minute. Would you mind first cashing the cheque that I've prepared for you on the desk? The bank will be closing soon."

Bent double, I shuffle papers in the depths of the cupboard. I hear Lucienne's steps muffled by the carpet as she approaches me. What if, moved by the idea of my departure, she wishes to feel her power once more and this time actually gives me an order? I'm afraid, and I'm tempted.

"Are you looking for something?" she asks. "I'm sure I could save you the trouble."

"No, thank you. I am looking for some notes I made about a month ago on the subject of purchases carried out in Romania by Poulet-Bichon. Perhaps I had a premonition of today's business. But I'm sure it will turn up. Go on, quickly."

"Of course. I do have time though. It's twenty-to."

She approaches again. I can hear her breathing.

"I beg you," I say, "don't make me die of nerves. The bank will close."

"I'm going."

She has left. I have at least ten minutes to myself. I sit down at my desk and allow myself the luxury of removing my hat, for I'm bathed in sweat. Passing my hand momentarily over my face, I am surprised by the shape of my nose. I hadn't forgotten the change wrought in me but rather its strangeness, as if this shocking experience were no more bizarre for me than my most familiar slippers. My hand's surprise revives my full awareness of the situation, though only briefly. Above all, I must face the problems of the moment, which are far from being solved, and as the memory of my metamorphosis catches up with me again I brush it aside with a movement of annoyance. In that perilous minute, the notion that I am living in 'the absurd' seems mere metaphysics. I want to deal with reality only in its narrowest and most immediate form.

I have gone abroad suddenly, spontaneously like this, several times in the past. Only three weeks ago I took a flight to London without taking the time even to go home first. My sudden departure for Bucharest should not therefore seem in the least suspicious to my secretary. Everything will be fine if I can only keep my face hidden from her now. In less than five minutes she will be back from the bank. How will I greet her? I'll have to speak at some length, give instructions, advice. But I cannot go on fumbling about in the cupboard. Besides, there will also be the moment of our farewells. None of that can be done with one's back turned. I had already thought of the boxroom, which has a door onto my office. It is a poky, windowless little room, about a metre-and-a-half wide and two metres deep. It's only dark, however, if one omits to turn on the electric bulb, a decision that would appear peculiar at the very least. Moreover, I can't see how to explain to Lucienne my presence in the box-room, where the cleaning woman stores her brooms and other cleaning utensils among the old boots, out-of-date newspapers and piles of interesting files on long-closed cases. I cudgel my brains, trying to squeeze out an idea, but nothing comes and I begin to panic. I resist the urge to snatch my hat and run away.

I hear the door on the stairwell open and close. Lucienne is in the vestibule. I dash into the boxroom and, heart racing, stand stock-still in the darkness, not daring to close the door on myself. She knocks. "Enter," I call. I am lost.

"There you are," says Lucienne. "Thirty-nine notes in thousands and ten in hundreds."

I imagine she's looking for me in the doorway of the open cupboard. I draw her attention to my real hiding place by coughing and making a broom fall over.

"Goodness, are you in the boxroom? But you haven't switched the light on."

Through the slightly open door, I can see the tall shape of Lucienne move around the desk and in my direction. I torture myself in horrified expectation, uselessly. It's too bad. I'm finished. This realisation releases me from a kind of interior pressure which until now has blocked my mind from working freely.

"Nobody fussed about paying you the money? Well done. I was half-expecting a telephone call from the bank. Well, isn't this ridiculous! The one time I enter this hole of a room, and the electricity cuts out. Never mind, it's not a problem. You know what I'm trying to do in here?"

"No. I am curious."

"I'm changing my underwear, because I'm not sure I'll have the time to go home before the flight. You see how sensible I am, always to keep spare underwear here to change into. So as not to waste time, I'll give you my last few instructions from in here. The darkness allows me to leave the door half-open."

I'm about to add "without compromising my decency", but I see that I have already protested too much. Like all people anxious not to draw attention to the strangeness of their conduct, I feel a powerful desire to explain mine and to dot every 'i' as I do so. I ought to have remembered that the most banal actions often have no obvious justification and that we pass over them with ease, each of us unconsciously relying on others' common sense. As for me, I have trouble relying on this assumption. A stingy kind of honesty, verging on meanness, makes me force myself to show my hand at every point, even when no one has asked me a word about what I'm up to. My cousin Hector, who's a well-educated boy with some good contacts in intellectual circles, frequently tells me I have a complex. If he's right, I will suffer from it now more than ever, as I feel as if I were smuggling in by the back door the little sense remaining to my life. However, Lucienne has come over and positioned herself by the boxroom door, leaning against the wall so that the straight part of her body comes a little way into the door's opening. She has taken a pencil and notepad from my desk, so as not to lose any of my speech that might be useful. I begin to talk about the main affairs in hand, starting with the meeting I have just missed. I abandon myself to this business talk with real pleasure, having no need in any part of it for cunning or restraint. I certainly make it more lively than usual. Old employees finishing their very last day of work before retirement must feel a similar exaltation. Never have I been so sharp nor so lucid. I find one after the other two practical solutions to a problem that Lucienne and I have been puzzling over for nearly a fortnight. She admires the clarity of my presentation of each deal, the forcefulness of my reasoning and a certain fluency of expression which is rare for me (I watch and analyse my performance constantly) but which I have now again tapped into. It isn't too much to say that Lucienne is quite bewitched, and this is even sweeter to me since it has nothing to do with my face. Almost imperceptibly and doubtless without intending to, she has pivoted on her feet by nearly a quarter-turn and, leaning against the door frame, she now entirely fills the narrow gap of the door's opening. In this three-quarter view, occasionally in profile, her whole silhouette appears back-lit and, invisible in my shadowy nook, I enjoy gazing at her without reserve. I am near enough to catch her honest smell of eau de Cologne and milky blonde hair, which always makes me think of a model farmer's wife or a Swedish gymnastics instructor. I have only to reach my hand out to touch her, and I don't resist. I take her arm, her waist, I draw her into the darkness. A curious thing: my spousal conscience doesn't trouble me at all and I forgive myself easily for forgetting my good resolutions, thinking that before leaving this young woman for ever, I owe her a tender farewell. Besides, following the massive transformation I have experienced, I may no longer claim to be guided by the same principles as before. If I wish my exile to be anything less than absolute, I shall have to resign myself to adopting a slightly different kind of morality, something more akin to that of a fare-dodger.

Lucienne however draws her face back from mine and, with a firm gesture, begins to disentangle herself, pronouncing with the greatest composure:

"You must not make yourself late. It is at least a quarter-past four."

I protest that it doesn't matter and that right now business is the last thing I care about. As she resists me, trying to back out of the boxroom, I slam the door closed on us both and we are left in total darkness.

"Do be sensible," says Lucienne. "we can't just go back every few weeks on what we agreed, supposedly once and for all."

She tries to push me away decisively. I clasp her to my chest, pinning her arms beneath mine. As strong as a man, she manages to free both hands and systematically resists my efforts. The sudden ring of the telephone in my office separates us abruptly.

"Go and answer it," I say softly. "Tell them I'm away from the office and come back here."

Lucienne opens the door having promised nothing. She perches on the corner of the desk, next to the forty thousand francs, and picks up the telephone. I cannot help but continue to admire her sound body and fresh colour.

"It is Mme Cérusier, wanting to speak to you," she says, turning towards my hiding place.

There is not the slightest hint of irony in her words; for a moment I am off-guard.

"Tell her I'm coming in a minute."

Lucienne passes on the message, then retires discreetly, without the least air of triumph. I will not see her again, for I plan to take advantage of her absence and disappear too, as soon as I have spoken to Renée.

"Hello, Raoul? I'm in Saint-Germain, with the children. I'm calling because it's already half-past four and Uncle Antonin still wants to drive us to Pontoise to meet some old friends. I'm afraid that will make us rather late. What do you think?"

"It is quite far away. At any rate, don't worry about me. I'm catching an aeroplane to Bucharest in forty-five minutes."

Upset, Renée stifles an exclamation. I give her the reasons for my journey.

"Are you sure," she asks, "that you're not getting into something dangerous?"

Her anxiety moves me. In it I recognise the orderly wife whose sense and thriftiness are my pride and joy. Darling Renée. I have never made a single investment without consulting her and have always found her advice sound. When I think that only a moment ago I was embracing my secretary in the darkness, a blush of shame rises in my face. I really am a sorry character of a man. If it weren't for the fear of hurting her, I would tell my wife everything. It's a remarkable thing that hearing her voice is enough to awake a craving for purity in me. She speaks, and straight away all the women's faces, legs, blonde curls and backsides that float through my mind shrink and shrivel away to nothing, as if simmered away in a saucepan. Dear Renée. Never again will I allow myself to play these revolting games the memory of which, within a minute of their happening, humiliates and fills me with fear. It's in the very moment of losing you that I understand the full splendour of my duty of faithfulness.

Renée asks me if I expect to be away a long time. That depends on how my new venture progresses over there. I cannot say anything for sure. I'll do all I can to make my stay brief. Besides, I'll write very regularly (which is easy to promise). Renée sniffs. Poor darling, and me too. Kiss the children for me. My throat is constricted. Before tearing myself away from the telephone, I bawl into the receiver, "Darling!" I pocket the forty thousand francs left on the desk by Lucienne and it is as if I am stealing from myself.

IV

AFTER LEAVING MY OFFICE with all the elaborate precautions of a thief, I decided to go back home, calculating that the maid will not have failed to take advantage of my wife's absence and abandon the house herself. It was in the taxi on the way to Rue Caulaincourt that the idea of seducing Renée first occurred to me. The failure of such a project seemed to me quite assured, but with a little luck I might get her to accept a discreet friendship. Women are often grateful to those who give them occasion to show off their virtuousness. And later, in two or three years, when the memory of her husband would, despite everything, be somewhat dulled, perhaps Renée would come to think of providing a father for her children.

As I had foreseen, the maid was not at the apartment. I could pick up underwear, toiletries and a suit without fear of disturbance. On leaving the block, I noticed a sign above the door which read '*Apartment for Rent*' and, beneath these three words, '*Furnished*' added in pencil. I went straight to Café Manière, the largest café on Rue Caulaincourt, and left my suitcase, overcoat and hat there with the proprietor. The air was mild enough for me to go out without hat and coat. This precaution turned out to be unnecessary, for I was almost certain that the concierge hadn't seen me enter or leave the building. It was half-past five when I knocked at her door. She took me up to look around the furnished apartment on the fifth floor—that is, the floor above my own—and at six o'clock I was settling into my new residence under the attractive new name of Roland Colbert (which allowed me to keep the same initials). The nine hundred francs a month rent that I agreed to pay was reasonable. The apartment, made up of three rooms, plus kitchen and bathroom, was comfortably furnished and in much better taste than my own. From my bedroom window, looking out on the street, I had a clear view of the wide balcony belonging to the apartment below, on which I had strolled that very morning after breakfast, smoking a cigarette, and on which I now saw Toinette's overstuffed rag doll lying forgotten. If I leant right out, I could just see the far corner of our bedroom carpet, which extended right underneath me. Later on, I suffered frequently from dreams like this: standing on the window ledge, I would back away from it into the empty air above the street, until I was far enough to see right into the fourth-floor apartment, but the blinds were mostly closed and I could see nothing, and I went on going backwards endlessly, right into the countryside, into the village where I was born. Or else I would wait for the blinds to rise, floating there above the street, and my weariness would make me swell to such a degree that I'd end up huge, overblown, scrofulous, and finally, trapped between two rows of houses, my life would be truly worthless.

For a moment or two, I shuffled idly from room to room, overcome by my situation. The furnishing must have been planned by a woman, for there was a profusion of conveniently placed mirrors. I could examine myself face on, at a three-quarter angle and in profile. I found myself less charming than I'd seemed in the little café on the Rue Saint-Honoré. All my facial features were very handsome and harmoniously arranged. But they lacked anything unexpected, any defect or flaw in the symmetry which would have given life to this rather lacklustre physiognomy. Perfection possesses a particular inflexibility that is not found in life and which stops it from ever being truly lifelike. I made an effort to laugh and smile at the mirror, directly and in profile, and my face lit up with a kind of syrupy distinction. It is true my heart wasn't in it. Yet even allowing for a certain level of mindlessness which necessarily showed in my forced expressions, I still found my languid gaze insufferable. "It's not with this manner that I could ever hope to appeal to Renée," I thought. "If she ever considered herself, poor darling, to have a preference for a certain type of man, she'd certainly not choose this one." And I missed the good old head I used to have, sulky, obstinate, unwelcoming, but in which all the features moved constantly with life and sensitivity to the smallest emotion.

Around quarter-to-seven I went out for a short walk in the neighbourhood, for I hoped to be there when Renée and the children returned. Rue Caulaincourt, with its sweeping curve down the flank of Montmartre, is the most beautiful street in Paris. It is quite a pathway to paradise, for it starts off at a graveyard, the Montmartre cemetery, then climbs gradually, curving, towards heaven, and its trees are naive and youthful all the year round. In this street's noblest section, that is, near the peak of its curve, it is crossed by no other street. For a distance of about two hundred metres without a single intersecting street, it is cloistered between two tall rows of houses with great arched façades. The stranger who strolls along this deep gorge hoping for nothing more than to arrive at the Sacré-Coeur shivers at the sense that a spell may have been cast on the surroundings, and asks his way with a touching humility. Two lines of cars stretch the length of the pavements following the street's curve, and seem constantly to meet at the next turn of the road. These cars belong to the wealthy residents, who leave them like this outside their houses while they take their dogs to urinate on the steps of poorer shopkeepers' boutiques; this in order to show themselves off to the grocers and butchers, and for their personal pleasure. A rare peculiarity, perhaps a unique one in these northern parts of Paris: these gorge-dwellers have not a single café, not even a newsagent, of their own. They must climb as far as Café Manière for a drink, where the road breaks from its confines and opens out, letting its trees mingle with those of Avenue Junot, widening, taking in open spaces. It is here at this crossroads that I have been living for the last dozen years, with my family.

I wandered down to Paul's, the big café at the Lamarck junction, after which Rue Caulaincourt changes its style, and mixes quite familiarly with other streets of the neighbourhood. The people who would normally greet me here don't recognise me, but in the sweetness of this autumn evening, places and objects remain loyal. I mean that I was not in the least disoriented but fell without

43

hesitation into my customary patterns of strolling, with the same interest in the same shops and scenes. I noticed this eventually, after I'd been standing deep in contemplation for several minutes at the foot of the Rue des Saules's steep rise, which has always seemed to me like a beautiful Japanese landscape, and so true to life that I can almost see a snowy crater shining in the background. I thought then that altogether, with the Rue des Saules and the shop windows, I was thinking in the same way I always had and that in fact not much had changed in me at all. Only my household was now divided, due to my having moved to the floor above that of my family. In two or three years' time, when I had found myself a sufficiently lucrative position, one worthy of tempting a cautious mother, and when, become once more by a different name my wife's husband, I would rejoin the inhabitants of the fourth floor, then everything would be as if nothing at all odd had happened.

Reassured and less mindful of my ill fortune, I retraced my steps. The light was fading. Ladies were returning home carrying boxes of eggs. Some of them were pretty, but the men didn't see it, for their heads were buried in newspapers whose enormous headlines made their eyes strain and pop. For my part, having read nothing yet, I noticed that several of the girls seemed to admire me, even turning to watch me pass. At the corner building that juts out over the junction of Avenue Junot and Rue Caulaincourt like a ship's prow, a young woman I had often seen in the neighbourhood turned off before me. Brown-haired, with dark eyes, a well-formed bust and hips, she moved as if belted and cambered and her legs were shapely. I had come across her only the day before, and, as always, watched her slyly. She hadn't even glanced at me. She never did. Occasionally, I nearly said something brutal. When thoughts of these encounters came to me at other times—and they did so rarely—I called her the Sarrazine, probably because of her black eyes and the subtle sway of her hips. And yet this evening, as she was turning into Caulaincourt, the Sarrazine looked at me, and not by chance but several times and purposefully. Her gaze, responding suddenly to so many silent questions, brought the blood to my face. For a moment, the Sarrazine was walking at my side, and as she discreetly took in my features I felt I should say something to her, but the thought of my wife kept me mute. I allowed her to overtake me, watched her walk on towards Manière's, then turned back the way I had come. Reflecting later on the incident, I understood how my charming new face might become a source of trouble. The discipline I used to impose on myself no longer applied. I felt a little silly. The poor man may well boast of his virtue in the face of the temptations to which rich people succumb. In truth, he has no idea what it is to be tempted to misuse one's wealth. There are at least two levels of temptation, the second being on a par with hell. When I used to be ugly, or rather, had a common kind of face, I was proud to think I was beyond the Sarrazine's grasp. I had thought I was successfully conquering my agitation, when in fact our encounters could never have gone further.

It was getting late and still my wife had not returned. The glow of the street lamps overlaid the last gleams of daylight and passers-by were few. I stepped inside the Rêve, a narrow-fronted café which looks out over the two roads. Sitting there by the window, I was sure not to miss my wife's return.

I used never to enter the Rêve without a certain distaste, for one is surrounded by a clientele that smells of sweat and thinks nothing of downing one with the landlord. Chance having introduced me to some of the local artists, I used sometimes to follow them here and have a drink with them at the bar. I didn't like the place, but I liked boasting about drinking there to my friends; it was an opportunity for them to hear that I knew famous artists and had myself reached a sufficient level to frequent the Rêve without risking being taken for some kind of salesman or a chauffeur in civvies. In summer, when we had guests, Renée never forgot to take them onto the balcony and show them the café with its tiny terrace, and to say laughing: "There you see my husband's club. This is the lovely establishment where he can be found propping up the bar with his artists." And the guests would fall about laughing, as if the idea of my presence at the Rêve inspired visions of the most hilarious incongruity. I laughed with them.

Finding nowhere to seat myself comfortably, I ordered a drink at the bar. Beside me, Joubert, a sculptor from Rue Girardon, was conversing with a man called Garnier, a tenant from my building. I listened distractedly to their conversation, for I was concentrating on the street outside. While they chatted, my two neighbours also let their eyes wander over the street scene, so they too saw our maid pass in her white apron, heading home with a paper parcel of ham, or perhaps some grated gruyère.

"See there," said Joubert, the sculptor, "it's Cérusier's maid. Talking of which, what's happened to Cérusier these days, poor chap?"

"Poor?" objected Garnier. "He's got nothing to complain of."

"I don't say he's got anything to complain about, but he's a poor chap all the same."

His words aside, the tone of his comments expressed a deep sympathy for me. This time Garnier did not protest, but did not bother to agree either. He was a short, slight man, with hollow cheeks and lively, honest eyes. Although he lived on the same floor as me, I hardly saw him there, for he was stage manager at a theatre and rarely at home between six in the evening and midnight. He had always been friendly. Quite clearly, he thought Joubert's pronouncement self-evident. A chilling sensation, a kind of dizziness, swept over me.

Just then, I saw Uncle Antonin's car drive around the square before stopping in front of me, and I left the café. Disturbed by what I had just heard, I unintentionally took Joubert's newspaper with me from the bar. It was to do me valuable service. The sight of his car, which had caused Renée and me much embarrassment in the past, this time gave me unmitigated pleasure. Hidden behind Joubert's paper, which I was pretending to read, I smiled tenderly. Uncle Antonin, one of my wife's uncles, kept a piggery in Chatou and was obsessed with building his own automobiles out of parts bought at the junkyard. For two or three thousand francs, he boasted, he could make a car that was "smart, robust, economical and in many aspects superior to a number of factory-made models". Uncle was a charming man and loved us all sincerely, but Renée kept him at a certain distance so that his untrustworthy rattletraps would not come too often to our neighbours' notice. Renée always had an architectural idea of society, especially when it came to the family. Given the money I earned she acted on the whole very sensibly, arranging our lives down to the smallest details, from the plates on which we served lamb to the make of my garters, so that all would be worthy of our station. For example, Renée would not allow me to buy a car, because we hadn't the means to buy a fourteen-horsepower model and she thought it hardly dignified to drive anything more modest. Such concerns may seem mean, ridiculous, even odious to people like Garnier and the sculptor Joubert, but even today, I'm almost certain that such people are wrong. It is these concerns that give life its distinctive bitter flavour, the taste of those domestic resentments which fester inside us and, perhaps even on our deathbeds, will come to hold all our certainties. Far from imagining that his niece could be at all bothered by driving in a car of less than fourteen horsepower, Uncle Antonin used innocently to call her every week to suggest taking the family out in his latest creation. We were obliged to accept at least once a year. Poor Renée. Everything that the comic genius of American cinema could dream up in the way of old wrecks was surpassed by Uncle Antonin's inventions.

In fact, he never had more than the one old car, to which he was constantly adding parts and making improvements and of which he himself observed that it metamorphosed faster than a three-month-old piglet. One of the secrets of these masterpieces of comedy lay in the contrast between the uncle's ambitious plans and the humble resources he drew on to realise them. When Antonin came to visit, it was not unusual to see crowds gather round his vehicle. Renée suffered terribly at this. In order to diminish the scandal, she had spread a rumour in the building and the neighbourhood, via the concierge, that the owner of this curious conveyance was a very rich man, an old bachelor, a little odd but also an artist.

The uncle's latest rattletrap was in no way inferior to its forebears. Its most striking feature seemed to me the way that its back wheels were a great deal bigger than the front ones. Uncle Antonin stepped out, his face alive with greetings, his long moustache floating suavely in the evening air, and standing on tiptoe in order to reach a porthole that served as a door to the back seat, he cried in a voice that boomed out into the street, "Don't move a muscle!" and stationed himself in front of the car, but without hurrying, for his arrival had not passed unnoticed. Windows were opening in the upper floors of the house and the first little group of inquisitives was gathering on the pavement. I too had stopped, keen not to miss any of the show, for I knew that the most surprising flourishes were generally reserved for arrivals and departures. Having assessed the size of his audience, the good uncle leapt astride the bonnet so that he was facing the windscreen and, for the benefit of passengers who remained invisible inside the car, gave a big smile and a gesture of encouragement.

"If it looks as though I have decided to sit on my bonnet as if it were a horse," he explained to the spectators, "it is simply that I need to reach two cords that are on either side of the engine."

He dipped his nose towards the windscreen, but thinking better of this, said:

"These two cords, furthermore, may be pulled one after the other. The sought-after result will then occur in two stages. But it is more impressive all at once."

Once again he leant right down, his arms flung wide as if to embrace the whole car. Soon a loud rattling sound drowned out that of the still-running motor. Suddenly the car's hood, a kind of black waterproof canvas stretched over arched supports, folded down at the front of the car like the bellows of a camera, while at the back, the far side of the bodywork, a vertical panel made from the same material disappeared neatly from view. And so my family were revealed, as still as statues in accordance with Uncle's order. My son Lucien was in front, and my wife, with Toinette and Uncle's dog, was perched on a kind of elevated buttress, for due to the height of the wheels, the back half of the car was considerably raised, to the extent that it would have been dangerous for Renée to descend by herself. A murmur of amusement rose from the onlookers, and I couldn't help but join in. Uncle Antonin's industriousness made me forget my emotion at my wife's return. Besides, I felt that lightness of heart which is well-known to men who have escaped their wives' control for a few days, and I laughed easily. And yet I understood and sympathised with Renée's sense of martyrdom. The dear soul, imprisoned on her platform, blushing under the gaze of all Rue Caulaincourt, didn't even dare to turn her head. Eventually, Uncle came to her rescue. Pressing yet another trigger, he made another panel swing open from which a little stepladder unfolded.

"Simple, isn't it?" he remarked, turning to the crowd. "Yet other cars have nothing like it."

Renée nervously kept the children close with brief admonishments, and avoided looking around her. My plan in waiting for her return had been to manoeuvre so as to find myself accompanying her in the lift and, from this point of introduction, become acquainted, at least by sight. I wisely gave up that plan. She would never have forgiven me for catching her perched in Uncle's fantasy of a car. I hid behind my newspaper, feeling sorry to have not even caught her eye. She was already at the front door with the children when I fell victim to an unexpected attack. Texas the dog, who was following them a few steps behind, scented me and leapt at me, eager to lick my face.

"There's an animal who's taken to you," observed Uncle Antonin, taking the dog by his collar. "It's quite unusual for him too. Sometimes he scarcely seems to trust me, his own master."

Uncle said his goodbyes in the entrance hall. I saw the children hanging on to his neck in such affectionate spirit that I felt almost jealous. But Renée drew the little group further into the hallway, for it wasn't right to let passers-by look in on family embraces. I couldn't see them any longer, but I could still hear Uncle's booming voice, even over the concierge's wireless.

"I'll come and pick you up on Sunday morning," he was saying. "Don't say no, my dear. Your husband's absence presents me with certain responsibilities. Besides, you've nothing to fuss about when you're with me. So, it's agreed. What? For the love of God, because I tell you it's agreed. I would be happy to come earlier, but I'll need some time to refurbish my car. The fold-back convertible roof is really charming in the summer months ... "

As he left the hallway and reached the avenue's trees, Uncle spat into mid-air. He had aimed at a branch and, having missed it due to its height, he tried again. Red-faced and eyes flaming, he made four attempts. Finally he stopped to get his breath back and, seeing me standing near his car, said:

"I made it, in the end. It's curious, I don't know if you've noticed; there are days when one can't seem to do things."

"It's not easy either," I observed, trying to disguise my voice.

"That's true. Especially for me, since I'm a morning man really. Ah, you should see me in the morning. In the morning I can spit to incredible heights. But tell me, can I offer you a lift? I'm going back to Chatou, via the Place de l'Étoile. Naturally, if you're going somewhere in town, I could make a detour."

"You are very kind," I said. "I was just going to ask if you were heading anywhere near the Place de l'Étoile."

V

THE OLD CAR DREW UP alongside the pavement, which also served as a bridle-path. Apart from a few cars heading out of town, the Avenue du Bois no longer showed any signs of life, and the path next to it was deserted.

"It isn't," I said, "that I want to get out here. But I'd like to say something to you in confidence."

With these words I let my natural voice take over. Uncle was astonished, and switched on a pocket torch to examine my face again.

"Good God," he said, "I could have sworn I just heard the voice of my nephew."

"Raoul's voice? Well, you are not mistaken. Uncle Antonin, I am indeed your nephew Raoul. Uncle Antonin, I swear it. I am Raoul Cérusier. Just now, you saw how Texas recognised me. It is I who married Renée Rabilleur, the daughter of your sister Thérèse. A terrible thing happened to me this afternoon. Suddenly, I don't know exactly when, my face was transformed."

"Well," murmured Uncle. "This is astounding."

"Uncle Antonin, you don't believe me."

"But of course I do, since you're telling me. I may still say that it's incredible. My word, do you expect me to say it's natural?" The uncle thought for a minute and conceded, nodding, "After all, it's not so extraordinary. Generally, metamorphoses come on imperceptibly, but they can also be quite devastating. In fact, I remember once my car ... "

As his way of explaining that what the industry of man can accomplish, God can do also but a thousand times better, Uncle recounted how he had, one April morning, so transformed his car that he had passed it in the street eleven times that afternoon without recognising it. And he described the car before and after the change, described the engine, glorified in technical terms the comforts of his invention and, so that I might appreciate the excellence of its acceleration, ended by driving us off again.

"By the way, where did you want to get out?" he enquired, as we entered the wood, for he had forgotten my metamorphosis. At which, I answered drily:

"Remember, I am your nephew Raoul."

Confused, Uncle excused himself and stopped the car by the lake. For my part, I was starting to regret that a need for freedom had driven me to confide in this excellent man. I wondered if his generosity and kindness were enough to protect my secret from his absent-mindedness.

"Your new head is not bad-looking," said Uncle, to make up for his mistake. "What does Renée think?"

"But she doesn't know about it!"

"Of course, you haven't had time. Let's go now and show her your face."

"Show her? But Uncle, it's not possible."

"Why?"

"Because she'll never believe that such a thing could happen."

"I believed it," Uncle retorted.

"Of course, but it's not the same thing."

"Right. I'm an idiot. Say it."

"On the contrary Uncle. It's quite the opposite in fact. How can I explain? The idea of confiding in you came to me just now when I saw you riding the car bonnet. Your eyes were laughing. The points of your beautiful long moustache were quivering like antennae. I felt that faced with a truth that was hard to believe, you were a man able to act in accordance with your own logic. I said to myself that what his heart accepts, Uncle Antonin allows. It is a rare disposition, rarer than we think. But what about poets, you'll say, well! For them, the absurd is moonshine, it's a ghost in a nightshirt, notions that shrink to nothing at the last moment. Poets slouch behind their common sense, making airs as if they're ignoring it, yet taking good care not to step on its tail. No, you might even be alone in this world. And as I like you sincerely, I told you everything. It makes me feel better, really calms my mind. Oh, I know you can't do anything for me. All I ask is that you don't betray me without meaning to, due to a moment's inattention. Keep hold of the idea that if I claimed publicly to be Raoul Cérusier, I would be locked up straight away."

"You take me for an imbecile," protested Uncle Antonin. "I understand perfectly that you're in a delicate situation. Don't worry, I'm not the kind who makes such a blunder. For instance, you're wrong to think I can't help you. You know what I'll do? I'll go and find Renée and tell her what's happened. She'll believe her own uncle."

It was increasingly obvious that I should expect enormous gaffes from the dear uncle. I grew desperate. I lost my temper.

"If ever you do such a thing, I'm taking a train abroad and abandoning everything. Understand once and for all that my transformation cannot be disclosed to anyone. It has to be like this, otherwise any tramp who's bumped off the Shah of Persia could take over the Shah's life and his belongings, any ne'er-do-well could insinuate himself into the bed of a pretty woman he desired."

"And yet, Raoul, the truth is the truth."

"Provided you can prove it, or perhaps just for the few willing to believe it. Of course, if two or three thousand people were to declare that my experience is genuine, I'm sure Renée would believe it too. I do know my wife. She just won't accept certainties that aren't acknowledged everywhere."

"Mustn't say that, Raoul, mustn't say that."

"All right, if we imagine that deep in her heart she's sure that I'm still her husband, then I'm almost certain she would pretend not to believe it. And she would be right. It's not in the contract. For other people, among our friends, it would look bad. For the children too. You can't bring children up thinking that the natural order of things can be reversed and that we have to allow for the absurd. No, believe me, you must for ever give up the idea of telling Renée or anyone else. Do you see what you will expose us to if you go on obstinately insisting that I am Raoul Cérusier? Maybe not padded cells, but prison for sure. There will be a search for the man concerned, he won't be found and they'll accuse us of having done him in."

Uncle Antonin sighed, shocked and discouraged by this vision of such a tightly woven world that left no room for truths of limited use.

"When I said that you can't do anything to help me," I added, "I was wrong. You will be my only place of refuge; you'll be the only one for whom I am still Raoul Cérusier. Look, I haven't even had half a day of this exile and already I needed to confide in you. And there's another side to my isolation. Here I am like a shipwreck survivor in a world that doesn't know me. It wouldn't be bad to have someone to vouch for me."

Uncle offered to have me to stay with him in Chatou. I would help him in raising the pigs, which were, he said, appealing creatures. As a crowning temptation, he promised to build me a five horsepower motorcar that would be so elegant, so comfortable … I thanked him and told him of the arrangements I had already made. He was very taken with my plan to seduce my wife, which he found irresistibly funny. His head thrown back, he let out his loudest guffaws, which rolled round the empty woods like a riotous harmonium in an empty church. And they went on! From time to time he paused for breath, then cried out as loudly as ever:

"It's priceless! Poor Renée, she'll have such a wild time falling into—whose arms? Why, her husband's! No, let me laugh."

And he was off again; nothing I did could calm his

hilarity. If I raised my voice, no good, he was laughing so loudly he couldn't hear a thing. Between us, we kicked up such a row that it was beginning to wake the swans on the great lake, and make me nervous. To the left of the car, I suddenly saw lights dimly reflected in the asphalt. I elbowed Uncle Antonin in the ribs, but too late. Two policemen on bicycles, attracted by the noise and the odd look of the car, drew up beside us.

"You haven't any sidelights," observed one of them, in an almost paternal tone of voice.

"Indeed, you're right," agreed Uncle. "When I stopped it was hardly dark and we were on a well-lit stretch."

The omission acknowledged, the policemen might perhaps have left, but Uncle, thinking once more of his niece, let out one last thunderous guffaw directly at the policeman who was still leaning down to talk to us.

"Show me your licence," he said, in a harder tone.

"Here," replied Uncle, with an aggressively sardonic air despite the fact that he was still fumbling in one of his inside pockets. Not finding his licence there, he explored the other pocket, then returned to the first, swearing between his teeth. I sensed the approach of catastrophe. Yet again, he had left his licence and registration book behind. We would be obliged to go the police station, where they would seize the chance to ask me for my papers and it would be a miracle if Uncle Antonin didn't make some remark to alert the police to my case. What demon had driven me to confide in someone? I foresaw my adventure's miserable end. Uncle was now on to his back trouser pocket and cursing, in a voice already raised, " ... the child of a devil who had mislaid his licence".

"Can't find it, sir?" asked the policeman, with sarcastic sympathy.

Contorted in his seat, one hand to his bottom and sweating as he struggled to unbutton his pocket, Uncle sat up on hearing this, eyes flaming, and roared:

"Your damn licence, you know what I'll do with your licence?"

He broke off. I prepared to fling open the door and sprint away into the thickest part of the wood. But his face spread suddenly with a wide smile. Drawing a card-holder from his back pocket, he resumed in casual style:

"You wanted my licence? Well, here is my licence."

After examining it, the policeman took some notes and informed us:

"You'll be fined for not carrying the necessary lights."

Another growl from Uncle. I kept him quiet by kicking him sharply in the leg and, once the police cyclists were gone, it was my turn to raise my voice:

"You do it on purpose don't you? Have you pledged to draw attention to me by every means? Are you set to ruin me? If I had known, Good God! Right, drive me to the Place de l'Étoile and we'll leave it there for now."

Uncle set off, looking sheepish. From time to time he glanced sideways at me, fearful and sorry, but I remained furious. Finally, he offered, timidly, to drive me all the way home.

"So that Renée or the children can see me get out of the car? That really takes the cake."

Still, I let him leave me at the bottom of Rue Caulain-court. As I began to walk up, he asked if he could count on seeing me again soon.

"Today," he admitted, "was one of my bad days. It's bad luck, that's all. But don't worry, my child. You'll see: I'm sure I'll think of some excellent ideas."

"Then wait for me to call you and we can discuss them. Above all, don't come to see me. I'll telephone you. And also don't forget that from now on my name is Roland Colbert."

As we were about to separate, he asked me if I needed any money. You have only to tell me. Goodbye Uncle. I set off up Rue Caulaincourt. Twisting and deep-set, sight of the sky here is rare and the street lights as sparse as on a country road. A few passers-by came into the circle cast by an electric lamp, disappeared into the night and reap-peared under another lamp. I told myself I was dreaming. The light in the street was like that in my dreams: neither of day nor of night, a denatured light in which things appeared faintly, as if seen through smoky glass. Ant-like, I made my way between two endless walls, for the perspective's finishing point drew back in pace with my movement along the rising curve, and this pursuit seem-ingly without progress was dreamlike too. Ultimately, my impossible metamorphosis was proof that I was dream-ing. If I put my hand out, I would find Renée's warm shoulder and, relieved from the weight of this horror, I would recognise my own bed through a haze of sleep. Nevertheless, I was hungry, and not too disappointed to see the lights of Café Manière appear above me.

As I entered the café's long, narrow dining room, I was a little dazzled by the life it contained, and at first saw only confused groups of people. Four or five tables were occupied. I sat down somewhere without thinking and having chosen my food I began, leaning on my elbows, to think of Renée and the children, who were dining only a hundred metres away and perhaps talking about my trip to Bucharest. My starter on the table, I began to notice my company. Nearby, a couple of middle-aged foreigners were dining, both sporting suits cut from some Central-European fabric. I recognised several local faces in the row of diners opposite. The artist Chasord, sitting among friends in his usual place, was amicably torment-ing a guest with questions at once innocent and insidious, whose undercurrent of irony further befuddled his victim. At the next table, people from the cinema were talking fade-outs and editing. Further away, the Sarrazine, sitting against the wall next to another young woman, was gaz-ing at me. Both were dining opposite a bald and corpulent man, who had his back to me. I focused on their group, taking care to look distant and distracted. For a second, I contemplated the Sarrazine, pretending not to notice the direction of her gaze, as if her figure were no more than an accessory to my meditation. She had a rounded face, to which conspicuous bone structure and a well-defined profile nevertheless gave a strong, even masculine silhouette, accentuated by the two symmetrical rolls of very black hair pinned high against her head. The black eyes had none of that softening moistness; their shine was hard as anthracite. Her solid bosom was dressed high, with a heavy lace corsage that seemed to be suspended there. The fellow opposite her could probably see right down it. Even while she ate and spoke, she never stopped looking at me. Sometimes she turned her head towards her neighbour, but her eyes did not leave me. Once, I made as if to answer her gaze. Her eyes shone even more brightly, and I felt suddenly a prisoner. She gave a little half-smile on seeing me blush and blushed slightly in her turn, but not out of timidity. People around us began to notice these exchanges. My eyes once more fixed on my plate, I tried to scold myself: Renée, the children, principles, my duty to my own self-respect, the danger involved in complicating a situation already tragic in its implications. But I could not stop myself from musing that I was free this evening, that nobody would ask me to account for my time. My wife's virtue even provided reasons to give in to temptation: in order to conquer her scruples, was it not important to acquire some technique as a seducer? Yet I retained some robust defences and my habits as a scrupulous and honest husband won out in the end. Having again caught the Sarrazine's eye without meaning to, or so I imagined, I turned mine on the neck of the man dining with her and examined him with an insistence intended to be aggressive. He must be rich, I judged, from the lustre of his white hair and the fine skin and English rosiness of his neck. A well-to-do gentleman with the means to keep a pretty girl. I thought I saw the Sarrazine briefly make a gesture of impatience, as if she had guessed the gist of my thoughts. Entirely satisfied, I returned to my food without meeting her eye again and began to read my newspaper. I had almost forgotten the young woman. They were just bringing my camembert when her two dining companions rose from their table. But she, I saw with a jolt like a motor kick-started, did not move: she lit a cigarette. "You're sure," asked the pink-necked man, "that you won't come to the theatre?" She pleaded a headache. The others leant over the table and made quips I couldn't hear. She laughed with them, louder than them, and stayed. She watched them to the door, then, alone, she leant back, looking at me through slitted eyes, and blew a plume of smoke towards me that dispersed over my camembert. I've already said I had not become used to women going out of their way on my account. This direct summons turned me to jelly. My gaze began with the Sarrazine's ankles and ploughed slowly upwards as far as her anthracite eyes. I hurried through my supper. When I had finished, she left.

She strolled slowly on the pavement, under the trees of Rue Caulaincourt. I joined her, excusing myself awkwardly, saying that for the first time in my life, which was the truth, I was accosting a woman without her permission.

"Permission?" she smiled. "Of that you have plenty, by the manner in which I stared at you. I even hope you will succeed in forgetting that now. What is your name?"

She spoke with a voice that was somewhat harsh, exciting, and suggested remarkable self-control. I answered that my name was Roland Colbert and that I lived nearby. Since I began to divert the conversation on to the subject of the play she had missed, she observed:

"You don't much like to talk about yourself. Or about me. You don't even ask my name."

"Because I have already named you, long before today."

"Long before today? But I never saw you before this evening."

"And yet I know you. A fortnight ago, you were wearing an aubergine dress with white piping. You are called the Sarrazine, with a capital. Your real name?"

"For today, the Sarrazine. I think it suits me very well."

She laughed, showing two white rows of teeth, and squeezed my fingers hard in her gloved hand. We stopped beneath a tree. With a brusque word she stopped my advances and led the conversation her way. Her manner of expressing herself was independent, or rather that of an experienced single woman, though not vulgar. She looked at me with a sensual, sympathetic curiosity, without flirtation, treating me—although she was twenty-six years old and put me at thirty-two—like a young cousin who promises to be a source of fun, but whom she was nevertheless bound to look after, as the older child. I liked her taking me in hand. We went from tree to tree, making each a stopping point. She ended up talking to me—as something to review—of a certain disjunction between my behaviour and my physiognomy. Struck by this remark and disturbed, I stopped to answer her, when suddenly I heard the sharp, hurried step of a woman's high heels and, from the shadow where we were standing, I saw Renée coming down Rue Caulaincourt. She passed by without seeing us and, a little further on, crossed the road to the far pavement. Renée would never go out in the evening without me, or at least without my knowledge. The thought that she was taking advantage of a separation that was supposed to be a trial to her in order to meet a lover on the very first day, and that she was leaving our two children alone in the house, sent me into a transport of fury and disgust. The Sarrazine stared at me, shocked by my sudden silence and perhaps also by the expression on my face. I grasped her head quite brutally, and clasping her body and pressing her lips to mine with a murderer's impulsive violence, I said with my mouth on hers: "Tomorrow, at Manière. I have to go."

I walked in silence through the shadows. Ahead of me walked Renée on the other pavement. I did not let her out of my sight for a moment, listening to the sharp rap of her footsteps. Filthy insults rose to my mouth and once or twice a tender word too that died in a sob. She stopped at the bottom of Rue Caulaincourt and I saw her ring at a door. Relief filled me. With a light heart, I recognised the house of our friends, the Marions. I remembered that one of their children had just fallen sick. Doubtless they had called Renée or she them, and she was coming to visit the sick child. Happy and flooded with a tender remorse, I blamed myself for breeding suspicions of my perfect wife while I was myself so ready to fall into the arms of the first woman I found. I realised that I did not deserve to have Renée for my wife.

She stayed no longer than half-an-hour at the Marions. I allowed her to get ahead of me on Rue Caulaincourt and then, before we reached home, I lengthened my stride in order to reach the door with her. I opened it and made way for her without succeeding in drawing her attention to me at all. So present, and so inaccessible! I felt again, almost as vividly as at the start of the afternoon, the monstrousness of this adventure which already I was coming to accept, and the idea of that acceptance horrified me. She looked sad and preoccupied, which I attributed to my absence, and my throat grew tight with emotion. Before closing the lift doors, I asked which floor she wanted. As she answered the fourth, her cool, grey eyes rose to mine and it seemed that for a second she was studying my face. I remembered that my voice still held some familiar tone for her, even though the new configuration of my mouth and jaw gave me every facility to disguise it. But then, Renée was no longer looking at me. She went into our home. I went into mine.

VI

ON WAKING IN MY NEW LODGINGS, my first thought was to find a mirror. There I was with the same face as yesterday evening. Outside, the aspect was bleak: a fine rain alternating with chilly gusts of wind. I put my nose to the window several times without finding any of my family visible below on the fourth-floor balcony. As I finished dressing, I went over most of the ideas I had already had about my metamorphosis yesterday, and found myself then at the beginning of a long day and with little of interest to fill it. Having no means of engineering an encounter with my wife and being forced to rely on luck, I could not make this a project with which to busy myself. While I waited for the lucky circumstances that would bring us together, if indeed they ever arrived, Renée was as far from me as if I really had gone abroad. What I imagined of the everyday life going on in the fourth-floor apartment I could equally have conjured up from a hotel room in Bucharest. It even seemed after a while that the thought of this useless proximity was growing tiresome, even irritating, like a crossword clue that one has worried over for too long without finding any solution. The image of the Sarrazine, which I had already suppressed several times since waking, returned with greater insistence and I came to welcome the distraction. The arguments with which I had scolded myself the night before seemed much less solid in the morning. In my inhuman isolation, my condition of invisibility, the love of a woman came to seem a right and a necessity. I have already said, if I remember rightly, that I had always taken care to fulfil my duties as a man, and was much less skilful at forging compromises with my conscience. Here at the start of this confession, you might judge these tendencies rather superficial traits. On the contrary, I was that kind of man: vigorous, happily very ordinary, born for hard work, devotion, friendship, patriotic impulses, obedience, marriage; the kind that the double anarchy of idleness and singleness would instantly leave vulnerable to his evil demons. Above all the anarchy of being single. You had to be in my situation, I mean freed of the ties of marriage without ceasing to feel their continued existence, to understand what a man can owe to those ties. The despotism of his wife, who channels his energy, blinkers him, curbs his charming or useless quirks, nags him in the middle of his dangerous daydreams and in doing all this permits him to improve his skills in the game of earning money, is an incomparable service. I often used to ask myself why I had married Renée. She was pretty, but there are hundreds of pretty girls, and she wasn't wealthy. Apart from a few surprises that rarely coincide with the notion of starting a family, one doesn't fall in love after the age of twenty-five except when one chooses to. This in no way compromises the dignity of the marriage. The choice, which is of fundamental importance, implies a freedom of judgement which is hardly furthered in the heat of passion. In my new bachelor's apartment, I understood, without particularly thinking it through, that I had married in order to redress one aspect of my life, that part of me that remained undecided, changeable, dreamy, muddled, generous, prey to those demons that incite sons of good families to sign up on the side of disorder and ageing bachelors to rise at midnight and wander the streets. Taking advantage of a feeling she had inspired in me, I had chosen Renée in order to put her in charge of the keys to this cupboard of surprises, and now that my transformation brought all these possibilities back into play, I thought of the Sarrazine, of giving to her in turn those keys I feared to find back in my possession. What I had seen of her despotic character the day before made me all the more eager to let her take them.

I was dressed and ready at half-past eight, the time I would ordinarily leave to go to work. Despite having skipped my usual coffee, I was in no hurry to go outside where there was nothing for me to do. I explored the apartment's three rooms once more, so as to be familiar with all its resources. There were few books. In the drawing room the works of P Massillon and a *History of France* in twelve volumes by R P Daniel, all bound in calf, filled one row of the bookshelf, for the sole purpose of furnishing the room. I had hoped to find a good Dumas in the cupboard, but no luck. Noticing the telephone then, I made sure it was working and had the idea of calling Renée. After a few vocal exercises, I dialled the number.

"Hello," said Renée, and I in a high nasal voice:

"Montmartre thirty-two? You're connected."

A silence. I counted to twenty, then in my real voice, a little muffled, I answered:

"Hello, Renée? It's Raoul. I'm calling from Bucharest. A fine journey. Hello? I can't hear you very well."

"Oh, I'm glad you've called, darling. I was worried. That long journey in the aeroplane. You weren't ill?"

"Not for a second, darling. And the day out in that crazy car?"

"I could have done without it. Uncle Antonin called me this morning at six o'clock. To talk to me about you and some kind of change which might happen to you during your stay in Bucharest. I didn't understand a word he said."

"Poor man. I didn't want to tell you, but several times I've noticed that he seems to be losing his marbles. If he bothers you, just send him away. And the children, are they well?"

"They're well. This afternoon I plan to take them to the museum. If you knew how empty it is here in the apartment since you left ... Sweetheart, I think we've been talking a good while now. From Bucharest it must be quite expensive. Let's be sensible."

"You're right. Goodbye darling. I'll write to you."

This eye on the cost of our time spent talking, when she should have been taken up with her emotions, seemed rather penny-pinching to me, but was useful nevertheless. I felt as if called back to order, taken in hand and newly capable of concentrating on the practical problems posed by my metamorphosis. I was ashamed of having feared the boredom of a long day. Had I not better things to do than fill my head with women, even if one was my wife? The forty thousand francs that I had picked up yesterday and the sixty or so's worth of savings that Renée had to hand would not last for ever and the family would now be living at double the cost or nearly that. I would have to work hard to find myself a new position, without a moment's delay. Each minute is dear. I went down to Café Rêve, gulped down a coffee at the bar like a man in a hurry, and caught the bus. On the bus ride, I found myself a job. It was as clear as day: I had only to introduce myself to my secretary with a note of recommendation from my own hand and a job would be mine.

Around eleven o'clock, I made my way to my office. Lucienne was talking to a client and Mme Lagorge bid me resign myself to waiting patiently. It was a melancholy interval. I felt like a discharged colonel signing up again as a simple foot soldier. Mme Lagorge (who, due to her scrawniness, I sometimes called 'the dry gorge') directed a number of friendly smiles at me from her window, such as I felt she would reserve for only the most promising candidates. After half-an-hour I was shown into my office. Lucienne was just as I had seen her the day before, but with a happier expression, a brighter tone, no doubt because she was relieved, much as she liked her boss, not to have him breathing down her neck. I introduced myself and gave her the letter I had just written in the post office. She asked me to sit down and, having read the note, sat opposite me in the directorial armchair.

"I happened to meet my friend, M Cérusier, yesterday evening at Bourget's, where I was taking a cousin out for dinner. We chatted and I told him about the fix I'm in at the moment."

"Yes, and you wish to work on behalf of M Cérusier. On which concerns?"

"M Cérusier suggested I work on metals sales and also then on marketing for that sector."

"It would doubtless be better to keep to one thing, for the moment at least. Of course you will have an approximate idea of nature of the work. May I ask you what relevant experience you have had so far?"

I replied that I had been involved in selling textiles. Lucienne listened coldly, her eyes on her hands, playing with the letter opener. From her attitude I guessed at her stifled desire to be rid of me and repair what she evidently considered a regrettably charitable impulse towards a distant acquaintance on the part of her superior. My handsome, youthful face hardly inspired confidence in her. She had often heard me say that only very gifted characters can successfully handle both work and women. What's more, she thought rightly that a man with a negligible or mediocre business of his own might damage our business and that if he proved on the other hand too resourceful and handy, we risked him disappearing one day along with our best clients. Indeed, at this modest level, my metals business could only be profitable in one person's hands.

"All things considered," pronounced Lucienne, watching me carefully, "nothing particularly suits you to the kind of work we do here. I'm afraid that your short conversation with M Cérusier gave him time neither to brief you sufficiently, nor to inform himself of your capabilities."

I wanted to protest. Lucienne's voice hardened.

"You seem to believe that this post requires nothing

more than the resources of a travelling salesman. It is not that at all. We don't sell tons of metal as you would sell trinkets. You need to have contacts, to understand certain specialist fields. Before it can be profitable, this business requires long preparation. Even supposing you have the right aptitudes and a good deal of perseverance, you would have to wait six months and more for your first returns."

She paused to study the effect of her words. I admired her lucidity and more than that her doggedness in defending my interests. I replied, in spite of myself, my enthusiasm carefully suppressed:

"Of course."

Seeing me defeated by her first efforts, she looked at me with commiseration, but decided nevertheless to finish me off.

"Moreover," she went on, "the rates of commission you would receive here would be markedly lower than what you would expect; lower than they might be in a larger company than ours. Even should things work out for the very best, you still couldn't hope to make a living here. If you truly wish to work in this line of business, you would do much better with a company of larger means. I could even give you some guidance on this. I could do that right now. Would that suit you? I'm going to arrange a meeting for you with a manager at the Stube."

She was already reaching for the telephone. Logically I should have yielded to her, for I agreed with all her objections and had nothing of any worth to counter them, but I had to recover the situation somehow. I did it quite brusquely, for I was humiliated by the slight faith she had shown in my letter. I stopped her with a gesture and responded:

"I am still too much of a newcomer to this company fully to appreciate your points, but I promised M Cérusier my support. He does, I believe, say as much in his letter."

"Very well," said Lucienne without a blink. "When would you like to begin?"

"Today, if I may."

"Then I will give you a few useful tips. It won't take long."

On a piece of paper, she wrote down the names of the import companies to whom I would be selling merchandise, the top sales prices for each category and a few other minor details. In all, it scarcely took up more than half a page.

"There," she said, holding the paper out to me. "Now you can begin."

She rose. I remained seated.

"Excuse me," I said, "but I will need some information about your clients too."

"Clients we have already acquired cannot be within your remit. That would really be too easy an income."

"Without knowing which they are in advance, I risk trying to engage them not knowing they're already clients."

"I don't think so," said Lucienne with an ironic edge to her voice. "But you have only to keep me informed about your projects. I will tell you what you need to know."

From the far side of the desk, she made a movement in the direction of the door. I didn't move.

"Mademoiselle, may I know, in the event that one of my future clients were to ask you for information about me, whether you feel able to give a favourable account?"

That was stupid. Having the advantage of knowing her hand of cards as well as mine, I ought secretly to have been amused at my chilly welcome. But I had taken on my new character so wholeheartedly that Lucienne's defensive manner angered and irritated me.

"I don't understand your question," said Lucienne, flushing a little.

"It seems that M Cérusier's friends do not inspire much confidence in you," I explained, teasing her. "I confess, he had led me to expect a somewhat warmer welcome than this."

"I am only his secretary. It is not my place to encourage you."

The scornful look she shot at me on speaking these words infuriated me. I could no longer clearly distinguish my own personality. The misery of my transformation and that of the character I was acting merged in my mind and this half-willed confusion sparked in me the intense and painful feeling of an outcast. Doubtless, the frustration that I could not make myself known to this pretty girl whom I loved sincerely contributed to this sensation. With dignity, Lucienne walked slowly around the table, eyes fixed on the door to indicate that our meeting was over. Sensing my anger beating at my temple, and perhaps flashing from my eyes, I stood up before her muttering:

"There was no need to tell me that. No, it's not your position to revive the vocation of an unlucky man who has lost everything and has no more to hope for from his life. You are right, don't waste your sympathy on this unhappy, this miserable man. There's nothing to be gained by it. Brush him from your path by every means you can and if, by chance, he retains one piece of luck, one pathetic piece, do your best to rid him of it. Push him to desperation. Tell him: you have lost your wife, your children, your savings, you are penniless, jobless; well, gasp your last then, and not a cup of water, not a bone; you're less use than a dog, die, die, to the dump with you, you're nothing now, nothing at all."

The words caught in my throat, eventually died on my lips. Tears sprang to my eyes. I turned abruptly and rushed to the bay window where I wept great sobs that shook my whole body and ended in infantile whimpers. When I was much younger, I had heard people weeping in this way over the body of a dead relative being carried away for burial. My sobs went on for several minutes. It seemed as if my eyes would never be dry again. Besides, I was beginning to feel a new sense of well-being, a kind of restitution of my equilibrium, as if this terrible despair was proportionate to the strangeness of my adventure. Meanwhile, Lucienne had drawn near me in the bay and was standing in silence behind me. I heard her say softly:

"I was wrong. Please forgive me."

I did not answer straight away. I waited for two or three racking sobs to die away.

"I was wrong," she repeated. "Truly, I am furious with myself."

"No, I am the stupid one," I said without turning to see her. "You behaved as you ought."

"I ought not to have discouraged you as I did. There is no excuse."

And so we exchanged protestations, me sniffing and keeping my back to her all the time. I was ashamed of this fit of despair in which a good deal of acting had played its part. Eventually I turned round suddenly and strode across the office room to the door.

"I'm ashamed to have made such a spectacle of myself. Please let M Cérusier know that I have decided not to take on the project."

"Please," said Lucienne, who had followed me. "Please be generous; forget what just passed between us. I will not forgive myself for receiving you so meanly and M Cérusier will not forgive me either."

She had joined me at the door. Her lovely honest eyes were moist with pleading and tenderness. I looked down, as if deliberating.

"Come back to the office this afternoon or tomorrow. I will give you more detailed notes which will help you with the work. There's a trick in our business that is simply indispensable. You see," she added smiling, "I cannot acknowledge my mistake more plainly."

"If only I could be sure that you *were* wrong," I said softly. "Well, we'll see. Since you suggest it so charitably,

I will come back, but only when I have secured at least one new client for you."

We parted with a handshake full of emotion, and to which Lucienne gave an almost maternal affection. It was about midday. I had lunch in a nearby restaurant where I sometimes ate when I hadn't time to walk up to Montmartre. It was always crowded, mostly with businessmen from the neighbourhood whose habits at lunch were more or less fixed. I had ended up knowing some of them by sight and I never went in without exchanging a few pleasantries. I was sat at a small table whose nearest neighbour was a certain M Couesnon, with whom I had had business dealings the year before. He watched me pass without seeing me. Even while setting about my food with a good appetite, I thought back with a kind of horror to the scene I had just made in my office. What frightened me was less my crisis of weeping than the feminine skill with which I had manipulated Lucienne. Without precisely meaning to, I had played a very low game, the sly little game of the coquette who plays up her own disarming vulnerability, rendered even more touching by her pretty eyes, and wins over the protective instincts of the masculine heart. While I should have been annoyed at having to use this trick in the first instance, I had compounded it with another that was ultimately unnecessary and moreover suspicious. And I wondered to what new need this duplicity and basely feminine, dishonest behaviour were responding. Until this moment, I had always been a rather plodding kind of male, very conscious of my manly dignity, and had the idea come to me, even in an emergency, of utilising these dubious means—which had worked so well on Lucienne—I would have dismissed the idea as repugnant, being much more inclined to be their victim than their master. Still, my metamorphosis was only external, according to some fairly convincing signs. I had only to review my preferences, my tastes, my dislikes; whether it were about men or women, a question of politics, reading or cookery, nothing had changed. I was forced to believe then that this tendency so unlike my usual manly character had been latent in me before the metamorphosis, only hidden from my own understanding. My new face, or if you will, this new consciousness of my face, was only now waking in me a harmonic thus far buried, stifled in my life as a man by more acceptable impulses which had been more easily expressed. In short, what had just happened confirmed my thoughts of the day before. Between a person's face and his interior life there are indeed certain links and reactions, reflections of one upon the other. These thoughts made me fear for the future. When I had become more used to my new features, at what point would I ever stop along the disgraceful path I had started on today, at what degree of abjection? Stealthily, I examined the face of Couesnon, my neighbour at table: he had a great bony head with a powerful jaw, speckled with ginger hairs that had escaped the razor, and the look of a sly devil, with his foxy eyes and a finicky little nose. From our dealings, I knew him to be fierce, greedy, cunning, devoid of any scruples, but not fundamentally bad. I remembered seeing him in moods of melancholy abandon which inspired in him a kind of shamefaced generosity, as if his heart had had enough of acting in accord with his brutish face. Watching him eat, as he tyrannised the waiter with his arrogant demands, I attempted to imagine another face for him, one that might have liberated a better human being that lay dormant in the shadowy limbo of his consciousness.

On leaving the restaurant, thinking of the comfort of a friendly voice, I went to call Uncle Antonin.

"Hello," said Uncle. "Is that you, Raoul?"

"Yes, but you've already forgotten my rules. Once again, my name is Roland Colbert."

"Yes, of course, Laurent Gilbert. I hadn't forgotten, I just thought it wasn't important on the telephone. My dear, glad I can speak to you now. I have some news for you. This morning, I telephoned your wife."

"Yes, I know. She told me."

"She told you!"

"I telephoned her as if I were calling from Bucharest."

"Well," murmured Uncle Antonin, "what a brilliant idea. I would never have thought of it."

"An idea that gets me nowhere. But Uncle, I have something very important to ask you. Think carefully before you reply. It's this. What impression does my new face make on you?"

"An excellent one," Uncle replied without a second's reflection. "You look like a charming young man; what's more, you have a look, I don't quite know how to describe it. See, with the face you have now and the person that I know you to be fundamentally, you remind me of my car as she was last spring, when I'd just fitted her with a six-cylinder engine. I don't know if you can think back to how she was, elegant as can be, yet light too, and delicate. One would never have imagined she could carry such a powerful engine. And the truth is that one fine day everything did blow up. I don't know if I told you at the time. It was on the road to Orléans … "

"I know, you told me the story. But right now, I'm still thinking about your impression of me. Anything else?"

"Nothing new. Actually there is something. I was just explaining. A fantastic idea. My dear Raoul, I mean of course my dear Gontran, it'll make your jaw drop. It came to me this morning, at six o'clock, all of a sudden. I was thinking about you and I realised that the most shocking thing about the whole business is that your new face arrived so suddenly, in the blink of an eye, so to speak. That's what might appear incredible to Renée. But if, on the other hand, the transformation were to happen slowly, for example during the three or four weeks of your stay in Bucharest, it would be much easier to believe in it."

For a few seconds, I let myself be seduced by Uncle Antonin's logic, then I shrug my shoulders. The concept of measure does not apply to miracles of nature. It comes down to essentials. If, instead of being total, the metamorphosis had only affected the top half of my face, it would have been no less incredible, and it would make just as little difference if it happened in a month or a minute.

"So I called Renée," Uncle went on, "in order to suggest that she would find you somewhat changed on your return from abroad. Of course, I don't need to tell you that, for this first mention, I was treading very softly."

"So I imagine. You didn't think Renée might be surprised by your talent for second sight?"

"Well, I'm taking care not to predict anything exactly. I suggest certain things, that's all." And Uncle added with evident satisfaction: "Very casually, you understand."

I weighed up whether or not I should discourage him from pursuing this new idea. Worried by my silence, he asked:

"Aren't you happy about it?"

"Of course, Uncle, of course."

"The other thing I like about my idea is that it means you can drop your idea of seducing Renée. Good-looking boy as you are now, you would easily have succeeded, and for that poor girl it would have been a sad thing all the same, and for you too. So, you can give me carte blanche here, are we agreed?"

Poor man, he hasn't even thought that I am my wife's neighbour and that she will already have seen me a hundred times in the lift during the period of my supposed stay abroad. I refrain from telling him that, in a minute, I'll be off to the museum in the hope of making Renée's acquaintance.

VII

I WANDERED AMONG the skeletons of antediluvian monsters thinking that, according to the jurisdiction of science, their stories were less amazing than my own. And tickled by my idea, I gazed benevolently around at the great lizards and giant herbivores whose carcasses reminded me of a building site full of motorcar parts. I was conspicuously taking notes in my notebook, and every so often sketching the jaw of a brontosaurus or a pterodactyl's tibia, a performance which would, I hoped, pique my wife's interest and perhaps provide an opening to conversation. I was still wondering whether to call myself a naturalist or an architect looking for inspiration here among these monuments from the very earliest eras of life. The architectural profession, whose artistic character in no way lessens its dignity, would appeal to Renée. On the other hand, as a naturalist I could count on a certain favourable element of surprise, knowing that she invariably imagined this variety of scientist as an old man with long white hair and golden half-moon spectacles.

My children were the first to appear. They were gazing in awe at the thorax of a megatherium, which towered above them like a ship's keel.

"It's amazing," said Lucien just as I drew near. "When you think they only ate grass. And the females must have made just gallons of milk."

"The females?" asked Toinette, looking up at her twelve-year-old brother.

83

"Cows, if you prefer."

Here I took my chance to make my presence known.

"Indeed," I said, "the cows of that particular species were very good milkers. It has been calculated that they used to produce between twelve and fifteen hundred litres of milk per day."

Fate had made me a naturalist.

"Super!" exclaimed Lucien with a respectful appreciation intended more for the megatherium than for me. I sensed that both children had questions to ask me, but their timidity held them back. Toinette, hardly bothered by the size of the statistic, turned her pretty hazel eyes up to me and, seeing that I was looking at her affectionately, gave me a trusting smile. Suddenly I felt weak with emotion. I wished I could embrace them, and kiss their soft cheeks. In the house I was constantly busy with them, patient with their questions, helping with their schoolwork and joining in their games. On my arrival home from work, Toinette would leap up and dangle from my neck, her head level with mine and her legs clasped round my chest as if she were shimmying up a tree trunk – but now, never again; yet she was here in front of me.

I turned away from them to hide my distress and caught sight of Renée fifteen metres away, standing between the tall back limbs of the monster as if it were the entrance to a cathedral. She was deep in conversation with a person who was partly hidden from me by one of the giant's tibias. The presence of a third party threw my plans into disarray. On the off chance that something might be salvaged, I strolled up to my wife's side, taking notes as

I went. My moment was clearly past. The best I could do now would be to stroll on past Renée without appearing to notice her. At least if she recognised me I would have caught her attention. At the last second, I couldn't do it. I whipped a magnifying glass from my pocket and, without stopping to reflect on the paradoxical nature of my examining a megatherium with a magnifying glass, bent keenly over the skeleton's toes. When I straightened again, I found myself face to face with Uncle Antonin, who was, apparently innocently, attracted by my little charade. In the shock of the moment, he exclaimed:

"Well I never, here's Raoul."

"Raoul?" I shot back, glaring furiously at him.

"I meant to say Gontran," he backtracked, "but what are you up to in here?"

I would have liked to wipe him from the planet. I forced myself, nevertheless, to reply as courteously as possible.

"Sir, I beg your pardon, but my name is neither Raoul nor Gontran." And I added, turning to Renée with a purely friendly smile: "My name is Roland Colbert."

"That's it, of course. Laurent Volbert, but I wonder … "

Most likely deciding that my face probably ought to stay a secret from Renée and seeing all his plans in tatters, the uncle made a great gesture of hopelessness and set to swearing under his breath.

"But aren't you the eminent Professor Urusborg of Stockholm?" I asked. "In your last letter … "

"What? A professor? There's no professor here, only Uncle Antonin. Now that everything is shot to pieces, these little acts are completely pointless."

85

I marked my surprise at these words with a subtly raised eyebrow and made a show of wondering what approach I ought now to take. Eventually, I made a decision, as if the presence alone of this adorable woman could have prevented me from putting this boor in his place.

"Please excuse me," I said once more, addressing myself to Renée. "I am a naturalist and I had made a casual appointment to meet a Swedish colleague, whom I do not know by sight, here in the museum. You see now the source of my misunderstanding. I was confused."

Renée can do no less than protest hotly on my behalf.

"Your profession must be quite enchanting," she added in that worldly voice which used to irritate me when we were receiving guests. "Are you an expert in palaeontology?"

She was proud of this word, palaeontology, she'd just managed to pronounce. I saw by her little smile of respectful complicity and by her more relaxed tone that this mark of erudition was meant to put me at ease in my professional capacity.

"No, I very rarely stray into palaeontology, but I'm currently preparing a paper on what I term the evolution of vertebrates towards the state of omnivorousness. It's a thesis which could at first seem rather far-fetched to many, but my arguments are persuasive. I came, at any rate, to try to test some of my intuitions against the reality and I have to admit I'm not entirely satisfied by what I've found. But you seem very competent in these questions, Madame."

"Oh, quite competent … That's to say I do take a serious interest in them," replies Renée, who has never been able to tell a house bee from a bumblebee.

She is thrilled by the high opinion I seem to have of her knowledge, to the point that her cheeks are flushed with pleasure. I sense, with a certain apprehension, that she finds me attractive. Meanwhile, Uncle Antonin, who doubtless has not yet pardoned me for having spoilt his game, begins to mutter:

"Naturalist. As if he looks like one. I was on the right track. Naturalist."

"Uncle," Renée asks him, "would you check that the children haven't wandered too far?"

While he takes himself off still grumbling, she makes excuses for the familiarity with which he addressed me just now and for his ridiculous suggestions. She talks of her uncle's slight oddity of temperament and strives to find a reasonable explanation for it, one that doesn't reflect badly on the family. It isn't that Uncle is touched in the least … since she's struggling, I throw her a line.

"Your uncle seems to be quite a charming eccentric."

I've said just the right thing. Flattered, relieved, Renée recounts several anecdotes which indeed demonstrate Uncle's charming originality. All are more or less made up, from which I can see that she means to entertain me, for ordinarily she shows little taste for lies or exaggeration. I notice that she's made no mention of Uncle's car.

"You have a sweet style of narration which renders your uncle a charming figure indeed. But I must confess that I'm less curious about this excellent man than I am about yourself. I am sure we've met elsewhere. May I ask if you weren't at the Countess de Valdoie's cocktails yesterday?"

Regretfully, Renée replies that she wasn't there and I see by her eyes that she senses adventure begin to filter into her life. It's not that she's a snob—I wouldn't say that for the world—nor a silly romantic, but she likes marks of status, fine associations. Taking a lover would mean a great sacrifice in peace of mind, in moral scruples. For such a cost, her lover must come with considerable pedigree.

"I mention the cocktail party simply because it's the first social event I've attended since returning to Paris. I came back last week from Afghanistan."

This voyage, I see, further reinforces my position. I talk rather vaguely about Afghanistan when suddenly—I'm inspired, I remember. We met going up in a lift! All becomes clear and we realise that we are neighbours. My wife is somewhat troubled and annoyed by this slightly suspicious stroke of luck. I pretend also to feel a little nonplussed, as if I had just committed an indiscretion, and we are silent for a few seconds. I turn the conversation back to vertebrates, describing how the megatherium and other species were bound for extinction since the future was for the omnivore. I feel that Renée is watching me more attentively than she is listening. Her grey eyes, normally cold and lucid, are shining with a warm humid light that I've never seen in them before. In this gaze, charged with an ardent melancholy, I thought I could discern the fears of a woman of thirty-four who is no

longer certain of her beauty, for I am young and handsome. However, Renée is still pretty. Her fine features,
somewhat insipid at twenty, have only improved with the
years. Certain soft and childish lines are now refined,
while some parts that had been too thin only now showed
a becoming maturity. Overall, in both her features and
her neat silhouette, I read the balance of her faculties.
I read this too in the elegance of her dress, which owes
nothing to the caprice of fancy. But Uncle Antonin has
rejoined us, accompanied by the children. He seems
resigned to the wreck of his own plan, and instead is now
excessively keen to push us into each other's arms.

"Are you still talking about natural science? That's a
subject that really fascinates me. I must tell you that I'm
involved myself. Did my niece explain?"

"My uncle breeds livestock," Renée allows, not wishing
to be more precise.

"My stock is pigs, and I do have some magnificent specimens. You must come and see them one of these days.
Renée will bring you along, or rather, I will pick you all
up in my car. What d'you think, my dear?"

Furious, Renée objects to this indiscreet invitation. She
is humiliated to be the niece of a pig-breeder and I fear
that she may not pardon me this knowledge. I attempt to
put her at ease.

"That's a profession I know quite well, for it was my
father's; I sometimes even regret not having followed
him in it. Besides, the childhood years I passed in the
company of the animals helped a good deal in forming
my vocation as a naturalist."

This is inspired. Renée relaxes instantly, and her eyes express her admiration for the ease with which a young scientist, the darling of countesses, can admit the modesty of his origins. I even think that for her part she might no longer blush to admit to Uncle Antonin's old banger, which must be waiting out in the street. I politely evade the invitation extended to me to visit the piggery in Chatou, or rather, I accept with vague formulas, moving swiftly to talk of other things. I turn to the children, reporting to their laughing mother the conversation we've just had about the milking capacity of the megatherium. Toinette listens to me gravely and I wonder if my presence in the family group worries her in some way. Uncle Antonin envelops my wife and me in a tender gaze, heavy with complicity and with his increasingly impatient desire for us to get on with it. Occasionally, he forgets to address me formally, and he responds to Renée's astonishment at this with a wink denoting that he already considers me one of the family. I don't know what manner to adopt. While I'm turning to Lucien who's asking me about the likely date of the megatherium's disappearance, I hear Uncle Antonin murmur to Renée:

"That boy is in love with you. It's plain as can be. He's clearly suffering."

Renée denies it, but I miss most of what she says. I have a feeling that she's not displeased by the idea. When our eyes meet once more, I notice the lively glow in hers. I wonder what she reads in mine. As if there were not a second to lose, the uncle suggests taking the children home for tea and leaving us alone for an hour or two, he explains, so we can discuss our views on the evolution of vertebrates. This time Renée is about to become really angry, so I spare her by taking my leave. I feel her warm hand trembling in mine, ungloved just a moment ago, no doubt for me to admire it, for her hands are delicate and finely shaped. Maybe a dozen paces away, I cast a glance behind me. Her eyes are following me, and without the least guile, she smiles.

For want of anything better to do, I have settled in a café on the Boulevard Saint-Germain. I'll do nothing more with my afternoon, nor, it seems to me, with my life. For no good reason, my encounter with Renée has left a bitter aftertaste of despair. It's not that I'm horribly disillusioned by her readiness to cheat on me. I would suffer, rather, from not feeling this more bitterly. But this new oblique gaze which, courtesy of my metamorphosis, I have begun to train on the key elements of my life, chills me. I have seen the emptiness of my place under the sun and I have a feeling that things are almost always like this. Where I am not physically present, I no longer exist. This is clear. It's not even certain that my presence, when I was still visibly here, has ever made my existence properly concrete. One must have the leisure to examine one's life with a clear eye from beyond the tomb and have plumbed one's secrets like a stranger to think such foolish things. One has a wife, children, a profession, habits, in short a universe that is dense, opaque, at the centre of which one is established, encircled, known, and in a single stroke, one sees through it all as if it suddenly meant nothing at all. The wife and children are still there, but the universe that used to rotate around me has gone. I recall a notion that used to haunt me when I was about ten years old: the world is pretending to exist, with no other aim than to mislead me, and if I could turn round swiftly and suddenly enough, I would find only gaping nothingness behind me. Automatically I turn round, but not quickly enough, for I see mirrors, leather seats, customers and among them Julien Gauthier, whom I hadn't seen come in. It isn't pure coincidence, of course, that I've chosen this café, his second home. From the time when we were legal clerks together, Julien had had a room in a neighbouring hotel, and it was during long evenings spent here over milky coffees that he used to dream of other destinies. Now a man of the Right Bank and the Champs-Elysées, he likes to come here alone, especially in moments of insecurity. I watch him with a persistence that eventually draws his attention, and I see by his expression that he recognises in me the strange character who collared him yesterday on the Pont Royal. I have debated several times since yesterday whether, if we met again, I would talk to him, and each time I had decided no—but I rise despite my resolution. Julien watches me approach without showing the least surprise and greets me with a friendly air.

"M Julien Gauthier," I say, sitting down opposite him, "you must have come to some unfortunate conclusions about my behaviour yesterday afternoon and I owe you an explanation, but I would like first to ask a question. Does my voice not remind you of another voice that you know well?"

"Absolutely. You have just the voice of one of my friends. I noticed it yesterday."

"Did you not think that I also have the same build as your friend?"

"Dear God … well yes, just about. But the coincidence is nothing out of the ordinary."

"And this scar—what do you think?"

I show him an extended white comma of flesh in the palm of my left hand, the token remnant of a deep gash he had made aged fifteen, unintentionally, one day when we were alone in Master Lécorché's office. Umbrella in one hand, pen-holder in the other, we had been playing at fighting the famous duel of Jarnac. It was an episode from our time as clerks that I'd often referred to in later life with Julien, and he no more than I could have forgotten the shape of that scar. He looks at it coldly. I sense his wariness.

"To believe that a mere pen-holder made this gash," I say, "you had to have been there and seen it happen. I could swear the blood poured out for over a minute. A real stab in the back, wasn't it?"

Julien's face betrays keen curiosity and even surprise, but not the amazement I was counting on.

"What are you getting at?" he asks.

I hesitate. I would like to remind him of other tokens of our former intimacy as workmates, among which there are some only known to us two, but I feel that nothing will bear convincing witness to such improbable truth.

"What I'd like to tell you is so unbelievable that I prefer not to attempt it. Still, I would have liked to leave you with a different impression of me than that I must have created

93

yesterday on the bridge, although, in truth, it wasn't that which inspired me to confide in you."

"Do what you think best," said Julien affably. "I shouldn't like to be indiscreet, but I must admit I'd be disappointed by your silence."

I hesitate to unburden myself for a moment more, but the devil drives me on.

"Well, I suppose I haven't much to lose since you already believe you're dealing with a madman. Julien, what I'm going to tell you is absurd, monstrous: I am your friend Raoul Cérusier. When I ran into you yesterday, I had just then, without even knowing it myself, had a complete transformation happen to my face."

Julien hasn't even blinked yet and this worries me. I wish I could take back my words.

"Everything is possible," he responds politely.

"No, there's no way of believing me. Don't therefore say everything is possible. Do me at least the honour of reacting a little; ask me difficult questions. Consider me a lunatic but one capable of listening to reason. Who knows? You might cure me, convince me that I'm not Raoul Cérusier. What do you think of my voice and my scar?"

"Well, they are strange coincidences," Julien replies, joining in my game with barely disguised revulsion. "They don't prove anything."

"Just so, there is no proof. A moment ago I wanted to remind you of certain memories only we two could know about and then I thought: what good would they be? For you, they're simply proof that I'm well-informed. I'm sure you'd hardly be surprised if I were to remind you of an evening in this very café, when sitting at that little corner table we tossed dice for a cigar pinched from old Lécorché's cigar case. It was you who did the deed while I distracted the old man's attention by handing him a draft reply to a letter from old mother Francgodet reproaching him for favouring her cousin Maîtrot over her in the Chenevières' inheritance. We placed the cigar between us on top of an evening paper and we'd agreed that it would go to whichever one of us guessed the colour of the other's braces. You said mine were purple and I that yours were white. I won. On seeing that I actually wore cream-coloured braces you said to me: 'Raoul, I underestimated you.' "

Julien is following with little nods and his eyes narrow. I go on:

"I could reel off memories like that one all night, but I agree I'm wasting my time. Cérusier could have told anybody his life's story, in great detail even."

"Yet one shouldn't dismiss the strangeness of your tales out of hand. Even allowing that Cérusier has told them to you, it's disturbing."

"Even more disturbing, I think, would be to hear me answer your questions. I could, at a stretch, have learnt certain episodes from Cérusier's life in great detail, but not his whole life. Please question me."

"With pleasure. One morning then, studying in the absence of Master Lécorché, I showed in a solicitor from Château-Thierry, whose name I seem to have forgotten … "

"His name? Master Bourquin, perhaps?"

"That's it. Thinking me alone in the room, my friend Cérusier bursts in … "

"Runs in singing: 'Lawyers, lawyers, hang them high … let them swing until they die!' The poor solicitor from Château-Thierry dropped his pince-nez and you, feigning anger, you said to me: 'M Cérusier, in order to curb your taste for this puerility, I shall have to ask Master Lécorché to refuse your pay rise.' "

"That's right," murmurs Julien. "What about the Torcaillon dossier? There was something special about it … "

"Yes, a great spill of red ink had stained almost all the pages."

"More and more disturbing. I don't see the point in continuing. What if you tell me instead how you realised that your facial features had been transformed?"

Without waiting for more encouragement, I tell him of the incident of the photographs, my first fears, calmed by a wish for peace of mind up until our encounter on the Pont Royal. Julien follows me closely, at least as attentive to my face as to my words.

"And that is how I found myself all at once dispossessed of my own life—and of my friends too, Julien. If I've chosen to confide in you, if I've sought to convince you, it's because I need to regain a friend. This sudden solitude among people who no longer know you is a terrible thing. Julien, I cannot provide proof of what I'm saying; I could never provide sufficient proof for you. You have to come towards me at least a little. You could do it simply by asking yourself: 'And if he's telling the truth?' I beg you to think about it. Imagine for a second: your old friend trapped behind the face of a stranger.

Julien, I remember one day, in this same café, you said to me, dreaming of ways of abandoning your studies with Lécorché: 'I'll never have an adventure extraordinary enough to make up for these long years in high collars.' You see? The amazing adventure which you summoned as your revenge for those times, it's happened to me! Have you lost the power to see it, to understand it? Or is our friendship so rusty that it can't support this test? If we were twenty-five again, Julien, you would believe me. You would have believed me from the beginning."

My voice cracks with emotion and I sense that Julien Gauthier too is moved.

"Clearly," he says, "it would be an extraordinary experience, but however much I imagine of it, everything I imagine remains a 'what if'. I can't help it. What you're asking me is more than an act of faith, it's a transformation of my religion and God himself could ask nothing greater. At least one thing is clear to me; it's that you're a very unhappy man and I would like to help you. What can I do? This is what I've been asking myself since the start of our conversation. The best I can do, perhaps, is freely to express my thoughts about your case. Since you have chosen me as your confidant, my reasons may carry some weight with you."

"But I know them! They are everyone's reasons."

"Exactly. I fear you haven't taken the time to consider them. You claim to be Raoul Cérusier. As you yourself admit, you haven't any way of proving this, but you seem to have a number of delusions about the value of certain assumptions. For the impartial observer, there is only one coincidence—which could be the basis of your mistake—that is the resemblance of your voice to that of Cérusier."

"And the memories? I gave you such precise details."

"Cérusier could have kept a very detailed diary of his life and allowed it to come into your possession. Because of the similarity of your voices, you became interested in the diary and ended up identifying yourself with its author, to the point that you gave yourself a scar in your palm. Your face lacking any resemblance to that of Raoul, you then imagined a metamorphosis. Your case is not so strange, in the end. I think it's what the doctors call personality disorder."

"Are you suggesting I see a doctor?"

Julien does not reply immediately. He lowers his eyes and I hear in his voice a note of troubled caution.

"Perhaps you could do something better. If you could see Cérusier in front of you, I think you would be cured. Shall we arrange a meeting with him? Let's go and call him."

"Hopeless. They'll tell you he's gone to Bucharest."

"Come all the same, we'll see."

The tone is imperative. I suddenly understand that Julien suspects me of having done away with his friend, which would be perfectly possible if I had the kind of madness which he sees in me. We stand up together. He shows me the way with his hand and makes me walk in front of him. As we go down to the basement where there's a telephone, I think that I've forgotten to give him a sample of my handwriting, but I'll take care not to do that now. It would only damage my case further. Julien pushes me into the booth and hands me the telephone earpiece.

"M Cérusier left yesterday for Bucharest," Lucienne's voice informs us.

"I was meant to meet him last night," insists Julien. "I'm very surprised that he wouldn't have asked you to tell me of his departure. When did you see him?"

"He left the office at half-past four."

"Right. How long will he be away for?"

"Two weeks, perhaps three."

"When he returns, please tell him to call me as soon as possible. I have something of great importance to communicate. Thank you."

Visibly relieved of his fears, Julien replaces the handset and says as we leave the booth:

"I hope you're not going to accuse me of plotting with his secretary. So, you heard just as I did that my friend Cérusier was still in his office yesterday afternoon at half-past four, that is, more than an hour after our encounter on the Pont Royal. I leave you to draw your own conclusions."

I could explain that the secretary had been fooled by my performance but, only too happy to have come out of this so well, I feign confusion and humility. He is kind enough not to reproach me and satisfies himself with gently reminding me, in case I have not already understood, that if provoked he would not lose a second in warning his friend about me and my movements. Before leaving him, I force myself to leave him with an impression of having had to deal with a harmless madman, brought low by the abuse of literature and drugs. I think I succeeded.

After two hours of exhausting walking across Paris, I reach Manière's hoping to find the Sarrazine there, but I wait in vain for her. I dine alone, then go home, where as soon as I lie down I sink into horrifying nightmares. I am trying to pass myself off to my wife as my cousin Hector, and I'm on the point of convincing her when Julien and the Sarrazine discover that in fact I have Uncle Antonin's voice and the handwriting of the megatherium.

VIII

THE NEXT DAY I TOOK A TRAIN to Chatou intending to move in permanently with Uncle Antonin. The very thought of living in Paris in an isolation broken only by bitter ghosts, my head constantly occupied with finding ways of hiding my poor bones, made me feel ill. At around nine in the morning I stepped off the train at Chatou station and covered the three kilometres to the piggery on foot. Uncle greeted me light-heartedly. I found him busy repainting one panel of a delivery van on which he had marked, below his own name, the rubric: "Porkers for All Occasions". This little joke had come to him in the middle of the night, and had him in transports of infantile delight every time he thought about it. He had a hundred and one things to say, most importantly that Renée was completely smitten with me. After I'd left them in the museum, she had been angry, reproaching Uncle Antonin for having frightened me away, and anxious about the impression I must have of her and her family. Then, and to Uncle most tellingly of all, his niece had refused to return to Montmartre in his crazy car, of which she had allowed herself to speak in highly-coloured terms indeed.

"This isn't proof, Uncle. Besides, I'm almost certain now that I won't seduce Renée. It's a betrayal that appals me not a little and frightens me more. It may be tempting to snoop on my wife's heart like a spy, but I don't see that it will necessarily do me any good. The little I got from Renée yesterday showed me that. A household's happiness comes at the price of a shared blindness, of a peaceable willingness mutually to mislead one another. Couples are like the tracks of a railway; they run along side by side, preserving the gap between them, and if ever they happen to come together, the conjugal train flies off the rails. Why are you so keen for me to seduce Renée? To find out that one says to a lover things one will never say to a husband, and worse? I suspect that already, but I'm good at ignoring it and I prefer to go on in ignorance. And then, Uncle, all these subtle ways of penetrating God knows what pointless secrets that my peculiar situation furnishes—I'm sick and tired of them."

"That's a pity," said Uncle. "I had devised a great plan to ensure everybody's future happiness. You were to go to bed with your wife in the next few days and in a fortnight I was going to arrange a neat little suicide for Raoul. His hat and overcoat, with a letter in the pocket, were to be found one morning on one bank of the Seine. Thus we would find ourselves with a good woman suddenly desolate, wouldn't we, and two infants to raise. Kind-hearted, you turn up, you learn what has happened, and you say, my dear, I offer you my name and my fortune."

"I don't fancy widows thank you very much."

"I would give Renée her dowry and I'd look after the children while you two go on your honeymoon."

"Raoul Cérusier can no longer commit suicide; it would cause problems for me. Yesterday, after I left you, I did a foolish thing which now forces me to be more careful."

I relayed to him my conversation of the day before with Julien Gauthier. Uncle scolded me indignantly for not having given this shameful figure of a friend a good slap. Then he began to consider me with curiosity, playing with his moustache, tickling the insides of his ear with the one finely waxed tip. "Perhaps," he said suddenly, "perhaps he's actually right and you're not Raoul."

I felt the colour drain from my face and my heartbeat falter.

"No matter," Uncle went on, "it's not important. I say that, but I'm perfectly sure you *are* Raoul. As long as you're sincere that's enough for me. As for Renée, you keep thinking about it. A young woman whose husband is slow to return is always somewhat vulnerable. You understand that I'm completely certain of Renée's feelings, but at the end of the day if the worst comes to the worst, far better to have no regrets."

Uncle went back to his painting, talking of other things, but his verdict of my situation stayed with me. I returned to Paris the next morning. My day at Chatou had done me good. It had allowed me to escape from a loneliness without hope, made up of others' presence, of their lives that were so painfully close and so familiar yet not part of mine. More than anything, Uncle had a reassuring way of accepting my story without question. To listen to him, one would have thought that it was simply a case of a bothersome accident, one which moreover was already well on the way to being resolved into the everyday. The first thing I did on my return was telephone Lucienne to tell her the name of a potential client and then, this done, I paid a visit to the director of a factory that I had been meaning to call on for some time. I spent an hour in his office and was quite pleased to make a start on a significant deal. Following this, I introduced myself at another establishment in the neighbourhood, where I could obtain no more than vague promises. These two calls kept me in Clichy until one o'clock in the afternoon and kept me busy thinking about them for the rest of the day. Caught up in my work once more, I hardly gave a thought to my wife—and I forgot the Sarrazine. Without any effort on my part, my affairs were arranging themselves quite conveniently. It always pays to approach a difficult problem caused by emotional complications through the requirements of the day's demands. A man's work is a kind of unravelling of his inner self, a reflection that he projects into the world and which takes its shape from his life's objects and events. To work well is to live well. You shouldn't have to undergo sudden metamorphosis to realise this. The next day and during the days that followed, I set myself to working with the same patient determination which had kept me going through my life's most serious crises. In this often thankless labour, which I had to manage now without the authority of my name, I found if not quite the joy, still the equilibrium of the old days. The interruption of my ordinary life still filled my thoughts but distressed me less. I took a rather impassive stance on the whole drama, which allowed me to think of it with a certain distance, to reduce it to a kind of backdrop to the main action. Without questioning it, purely because all my work was for her and the children and because this exertion clearly obliged me to reconnect our lives, I had decided that Renée would be my mistress and, God permitting, my wife.

I met her several times in the next few days in the Rue Caulaincourt, near the house. I contented myself with a simple bow each time, putting all the passion I could muster into my melancholy eyes. She was grateful for my discretion, but as I was later to find she did not entirely trust me in this.

One afternoon, having learnt from Uncle Antonin that she had an errand near Madeleine, I posted myself by the shop door and approached her as she stepped outside. Her smile was warm but she gave me her hand with an air of haste and annoyance. It was touching to observe the embarrassment into which this unexpected encounter threw the normally self-possessed woman. Yet I was not embarrassed by emotion, nor even emotional enough. The idea that I was manipulating her, and the awareness of what she owed me as her husband, left my mind quite free. Renée was no longer a symbol of my absurd experience; she had become part of my working schedule, and I was merely smoothing out a small hiccup in my personal world in between two business meetings. Without awkwardness and as soon as our first pleas-antries had been exchanged, I spoke to her of my love, which I presented as something rational and dependable, on which I intended to focus all my bachelor's existence. I asked her pardon for offering what must be a secret love, but it was not my place to expose the union of our two hearts to the light of day. Luck was taking her time to step in here. Overcome, her cheeks flushed hot, Renée gazed at me in fearful belief, as if drinking in my words, and yet offering nothing on her part but excuses and objections.

"I am used to living without lies. I could not stand to hide something in my own home. I couldn't behave freely with my children, or freely with anyone, anywhere at all."

"I understand what you're saying. Yes, I'm asking a great deal of you—I understand, perhaps more than you do, how much this means. You are right to weigh up the advantages. Don't hurry to reply. Even if you're ready to tell me, I ask you to hold on for a couple of days. I would like to think that for those few days at least, you will be mistress of my life."

We part in eloquent silence. I turn to see Renée's delicate figure disappear among the passers-by. I cannot help thinking ruefully that we are playing an unequal game. The intoxication of adventure is hers alone. I reproach myself for not being even a little excited. A husband's imagination rarely meets such a good opportunity. Doubtless the trauma of my metamorphosis had already hardened me to exciting and unexpected situations. Whatever I do, I feel essentially a man of domestic pleasures and I'm afraid I lack a sense of romance. It's highly important for my plans that I be a peerless lover, or at least that I don't disappoint Renée.

In the evening I purchased several used Romanian stamps, some fancy writing paper, a pot of glue and the few other accessories of a forger. I wanted to create a letter addressed to Renée from Romania, which I would secretly slip into her post the next day. That evening, on leaving the restaurant—where the Sarrazine still had not made a second appearance—I set to work. My fabrication of a Romanian envelope was not the most delicate operation. I wanted to write a letter which, without rousing my wife's jealousy, would convey images of nights out, heavy drinking and masculine gaiety, and of an affectionate vulgarity which would lead to comparisons of little advantage to the absent husband. Here is one passage from it:

> *By midnight, we were all out among the vines. Old Brown was determined to draw a bell tower on the bottom of a fat girl who came with us. I've never laughed so much. Apparently I was the cause of some of the comedy, but I have to admit I don't remember much of it. You'll imagine that I'm living in quite dissipated style here, but don't worry darling. There's nothing beyond the stories I tell you. My good little angel, think to yourself that we're both old enough to confide everything to each other, whatever happens.*

Four days later, on a Monday afternoon, I met Renée in the lift again. We were alone, and I was determined. Monday could only be a good day to try out my plans, for lonely Sundays are poor encouragement to wives left at home. Renée didn't notice when I pressed the button for the fifth floor. As the lift rose from floor to floor, I said to her: "Renée, my heart is breaking, I suffer accursedly. Oh! Good God, Renée, I can't wait any longer to know your mind, I'm dying here before you."

All of this, well-rehearsed over the last couple of days, came out in a harsh croak. I had decided that I mustn't be afraid of melodrama, of the impassioned roar, that I should actively avoid that tepid, measured way of hinting at my love which I had thought elegant when we were engaged and which might have reminded her of that. Renée seized my hand and squeezed it hard, whispering my name. Then something quite unexpected happened. This happiness that I had predicted, hoped for, *relied on*, infuriated and saddened me. An impulse of anger, of jealous despair at this faithless wife swept over me. I took her by the shoulders, gripping hard enough to hurt her, and said in a wounded voice: "Renée, Renée, it's impossible." She misunderstood me. The lift stopped. I followed her onto the landing and opened the door to my apartment. It took her a second or two to realise that she had come to my floor and, shocked, her eyes frightened, she uttered a little "oh" and took a step back. "Someone might see you," I said. "Come in quickly." That decided her. The entrance hall was dark and, with the landing light behind her, I could scarcely see my wife's face. This was lucky, for I might otherwise have caught there a glow of tenderness and been provoked to curses or worse. Instead, as she took off her hat and went to lay it on a table, she made a charming gesture of renunciation, which forced a cry of sympathy from me. Slipping her arms around my neck, she pressed her face into my shoulder and said my love, my love, several times over. I just managed to hold in a grim laugh, I was on the verge of slapping her and yet I obeyed the requirements of the situation. I held Renée against my chest with a violence that could have been loving, which it was also. I remained silent, which did no harm either. My nose pressed into my wife's hair, I gazed at the knob on the door to the toilet. It's a sad situation all the same, I thought. I had trusted her blindly. I was frozen to the spot in my respect, in adoration of her. When I cheated on Renée, which was rarely, remorse would stop me sleeping, but as for her, the first idiot who turns up, a man she's not spent more than an hour with in her life, she jumps on his neck and calls him her love.

Yet, I had to do what was necessary. We couldn't stay in the hallway for ever. I drew her into the drawing room, bid her sit on the chaise longue above which were ranged the calfskin volumes of Massillon. What a charming apartment you have. I respond gruffly. But my righteous husband's anger is soon deflected. Renée has never looked so pretty, even in the time before our marriage. I try to convince myself that I haven't ever really seen her. A faithful and devoted husband, I had been living with a rather naive image of my wife, which had hidden her true beauty. Shared existence, the familiarity of a presence, such things may conceal great errors. But this evening, Renée truly was another woman, her face so transformed that I felt as if I saw her lit with passion for the first time, like a statue suddenly given life. It was the glow of her hidden life, unknown to me and perhaps even to her, which played subtly over her features, giving to each a new meaning, to the whole an unexpected harmony. Her eyes, ordinarily of a water both chill and clear, which her father sometimes called

her slave-driver's look, this evening had quite another
light, of an amazing, almost animal gentleness. Even her
voice was changed. Fearfully I caressed the great joy in
this woman, which struck echoes in me too and revealed
an answering happiness in me that was quite new. I was
dazzled in spite of myself, filled with the same ardent
tenderness that transformed Renée. I had believed I was
manipulating her and I found myself caught unawares.
For me, it was more than the rejuvenation of her presence: it was another love, a love in which everything was
new, which made me doubt I had ever really loved Renée
before. The sturdy, sincere emotion which I had claimed
for her till this moment now seemed brief, muddled,
almost silly—several times I even felt ashamed of it. In
one moment of exaltation, I even thought: God bless my
metamorphosis; perhaps this is only the beginning and
already I am in awe.

Our clothes lay flung together on a chair. Renée opened
her eyes and the blood returned to her pale cheeks. Wary
of my own astonishment, I feared she might faint away
like an illusion that my limp arms could no longer hold.
She stayed—even this was another marvel. Renée rested
her pensive eyes on my face, looking so grave she was
almost severe. Then, closing her eyes again, she put her
mouth to my ear and said softly:

"Roland, I had no idea. I knew nothing about love. I
swear it. Oh nothing! Nothing, nothing."

"Is that possible?" I whispered bitterly.

"Roland," she said again, still in her low voice, "I want
you to know why it is that I love you a thousand times

more than I did before coming here. What I had heard was love, I only felt as a burden."

"Renée don't say that. It's terrible."

"No, it's wonderful. If only you knew. One day, I'll tell you everything."

For the first time since I'd lived in this apartment, the telephone rang. Only Uncle Antonin had my number. The phone was in the other room and the partition wall was thin. I didn't move. Renée was surprised.

"Perhaps it's something important. Do go and answer it, I beg you."

I obeyed, reluctantly, moving with calculated slowness in the hope that Uncle would give up. I was wrong. That evening, he would have kept on till the last trumpet.

"Is that you Raoul? I mean to say, Gontran? It's your old Uncle here. I haven't heard a peep from you since you were at Chatou. I was worried."

"You know I'm very busy at the moment. My work on vertebrates takes up much of my time."

"What? Oh of course, the vertebrates," exclaimed Uncle with a loud chuckle. "Well, since I have you now, everything is fine. My dear, I'm very pleased, you know, and you will be too. Just think, this morning I had a stupendous idea. And right away everything's completely different. There's no longer any need for you to seduce poor little Renée, for one thing."

"Let's speak about it another time. At the moment I'm working on the capacity shown by certain vertebrates whose species has remained the same for a long period to adapt to their environment—I mean for example the lemur types, and the three-toed species. Of course you understand me?"

"What on earth are you jabbering on about? Why for pity's sake do you keep going on about vertebrates?"

"Because I'm obliged to. Look at primates and ovines. One is faced here with a case of automatic inhibitive reflex."

"Good God," exclaimed Uncle again, and lowering his voice, "she's there isn't she? She's in your apartment? Once again, you knock all my plans on the head. It's all over. I'm too late, aren't I?"

"Well, yes, too late, indeed."

"It's a base thing, Raoul, what you've just done. Poor sweetheart. Perhaps I should come and drop in on her tomorrow?"

"No, absolutely not. I shall take some time to think over your objections. Thank you, and good evening."

As I replace the handset, I take a moment to look at myself in the hall mirror, above the telephone. I look critically at my handsome eyes, to which I must attribute the miraculous change wrought in Renée and also this sudden kindling of desire. All it took was a new face, nothing but a mask. Is love such a thing of chance and so little grounded in reality that a face makes such a difference? Perhaps, after all, Renée will discover the man she used to know beneath this charming mask, and will soon feel nothing more for him than that placid, affectionate solidarity which has already sustained her through thirteen years of marriage. Some unfounded arrogance stops me believing this. There remains only the chance that she discover something, and even were she to learn the truth she would not return to reality without some trophy. Yet more than anything, I feel as if she has seen in me, far deeper than my face, untouched regions where I have yet to explore, a new sensitivity, perhaps even a new and subtler intelligence. Just now, with her there, I felt the truth of certain exchanges in which both beginning and end are within me, buried at unknown depths. Is it so surprising? I remember some thoughts I had the other day about the interdependence of one's face and one's interior life. If for me my soul is the expression of some relation between these two factors, why should it not be so also for those who look on me? I do believe that the so-called transparency of a face is no vain metaphor, that each man's face truly represents his soul, illuminating its appearance by that particular refractive index that is his due. This means of recognition has no trickery about it. The sun warms us and illumines us according to the state of the sky: whether it is clear or cloudy or hazy. So too our angle on the soul; when we can see it, we grasp it clearly.

Reflected in the mirror, I see Renée, with her coat thrown over her shoulders, open the door and step timidly into the open doorway. I ask her, "Were you anxious?" She says, "Yes."

"I couldn't hear you speaking any more. I was frightened. I began to tremble. First, I thought I was stupid, since you had been talking about vertebrates on the phone. But I began to imagine things. I thought I could see you thinking, with your chin in your hand. What are you doing, Roland?"

"I was looking at myself in the mirror. I wanted to see myself as you do."

"You couldn't. I see so far into your eyes."

IX

IF I HAD BEEN CERTAIN she would take me at my word, I wouldn't have dropped the slightest hint to Renée about my metamorphosis. One evening, I was sitting with Uncle Antonin in a café on Avenue Wagram.

"Now," he was saying, "that she is madly in love with you, you can make her believe whatever you like. Why don't you tell her the truth?"

I shook my head. My face suddenly flushed to my ears.

"The whole situation would be so much simpler for it," he continued. "Instead of wasting your time and energy separately trying to deceive everyone, you could work together and perhaps find a way to live as a proper family again. Hmm? Why not tell her everything?"

"Never!" I exclaimed, furious.

Uncle stared at me curiously.

"I see," he said, grinning. "The intimacy of lovers holds greater charm for you than that of married life."

"It isn't that at all. My greatest wish would be to live with her again, I assure you."

I'm not lying here, but I haven't said everything I'm thinking. He waits for me to go on. I avoid the main question, claiming that for Renée my metamorphosis is still an impossible fairy tale. I could tell the uncle the truth, but it touches on such private convictions that modesty holds me back. He would hardly understand that the idea of bringing back Raoul Cérusier horrifies me. He wouldn't understand that with each passing day my metamorphosis becomes more deeply part of me and that already I am a different man.

Of course, I don't pretend to have wiped out my old self entirely. I'm continually recognising my old ways of feeling, of thinking, but mostly these are doubled, somehow shadowed, with new reactions, still hesitant, sometimes showing only in furtive regrets, at other times clearly evident as powerful imperatives. The differences are subtle, altering minutely each time I try to examine them, and I can only note the changes in passing, never pin them down. I am more confident in my judgement when I analyse some fundamental element of my character, for example my sense of duty, which used to be unshakeable. I still had this, but it was so much more astute, more nuanced, critical and altogether less solid; I had several opportunities to notice it. Apart from this, I am quite suspicious of all these hidden changes and I try not to include new habits I might have adopted through suggestion. But certain findings don't mislead; it's impossible to see in these the work of one's imagination; this is how it is when a new emotion, a sensation or even a word which I've heard or spoken myself brings a sensation of physical well-being or of pain. Often, unintentionally, Renée contributes to these subtle discoveries.

I cannot help but assess some of my findings through my old eyes, and they disturb me. On one hand, I feel better-equipped to savour life; on the other I'm less well-armed against its luxuries. Still I regret nothing—on the contrary—and I cannot wait for my soul to catch up with the model proffered by my face.

Since Renée started coming to me I work less, for I devote most of my afternoons to her. I never feel the remorse which used to spoil time I took off work. My worker's conscience is scarcely troubled by it, nor is my paternal one. I've acquired the ability to distance myself easily from certain cares. They no longer haunt me as they used to, where I have no need of them. Besides, I have new, more selfish concerns: to know myself, to articulate what life might have to offer me, to keep myself constantly in that state of nervous abandon which makes me accessible to emotions and feelings. I really feel that my passion for Renée is exceptionally intense; I've never felt anything that comes close. Sometimes I even wish a chance would arise for me to give my life for her. And yet, I think of our love as a particular moment of my existence, a happiness I must draw on until it's used up. I don't forget that she is thirty-four years old. When I'm with her I sometimes imagine the terrible sorrow I shall one day cause her, and I love Renée all the more for it, which doesn't in the least prevent love's ending, or even put it off. I see my life go on, tormented and passionate, while hers slips away in a shadow of sadness. The children. I do not love them any less, but I'm becoming used to placing them outside my life's main imperative. What I used to consider my reason for living—which it really was—I now relegate to the margins of my existence. I reject all constraints which I used to accept happily.

Given the short period I devote to my work, I am getting fairly satisfactory results. With very reduced means, my productivity is at least as good as it was. Since I began my campaign as Roland Colbert, ten days ago, I've embarked on several new negotiations and three look like concluding soon, and I've nailed an important contract. I did no better before, despite working longer hours and in easier conditions. My success has nothing to do with a sharper business sense or a more subtle understanding of my clients' psychology. Besides, in my line of business, persuasion counts for little and you hardly have to sell the goods. Everything comes down to making an offer and providing very precise references for it. Normally, I never attempted a deal without numerous flattering recommendations intended to put me on a level with my host, and never on unprepared ground. Now my metamorphosis strips me of the advantage of my contacts and I can only mention them obliquely. My secret consists simply of interesting people in me, and I succeed in this almost without trying. People want to see me again; I'm invited to come back another time or for dinner. My new face obviously counts for something in all this, for it lends me an ease I never had before. Above all, people are interested in me because they sense that my own interest also lies in myself.

I was going to the office yesterday morning to give an account of the deal I had concluded the day before. I had not seen Lucienne since the day of the crying fit. She seemed less surprised by my reappearance than by a certain change that she saw in me. A few seconds ago, I

118

had telephoned her from Bucharest to ask her what she thought of my friend Roland Colbert. She had spoken of him with warmth and compassion and, sorry that he had not returned to the office, expressed almost maternal concerns for his well-being. The poor boy was not equipped to protect himself in such a difficult situation, no more than he was equipped to succeed in his chosen profession. She would have liked to see him again and try to point him in the right direction.

I saw straight away that she was disappointed in her desire to pity me. I was wearing a brand new suit, of rich fabric and unusual tailoring. I had come to tell her that I had succeeded, contrary to her predictions, in handling a deal. I attempted to revive her sympathy by presenting my success as due to her: "I was helped along by an extraordinary piece of luck, but I would never have been ready to take advantage of it if I'd not been heartened by the memory of your friendliness and generosity."

"Still, you haven't so much to be thankful for," Lucienne replied. "If I had been more understanding from the beginning, you would have been able to start work with some background information which would have simplified your job. I thought of sending it to you later on, but I didn't have your address."

"It's true, I forgot to give it to you. But that information, believe me, could hardly have been more useful to me than my desire to be worthy of your trust. I wanted so much to redeem myself in your eyes, to make you forget that silly, shameful scene I made last time I was here."

Touched by my humility, and flattered too by the importance I accorded her, Lucienne protested. And so I was wrong to return to the attack. Relying, in spite of myself, on her need to offer compassion and protection, I spoke at length about the uncertainty and the spinelessness which I felt formed the foundation of my character.

The indulgent way I spoke about myself, as well as this display of weakness, almost indecent in its pretentiousness, must have shocked Lucienne. I only thought of this after I'd left her. Thinking over my words, everything I'd just said—and I'd not been brief—sounded false, like a stodgy literary confession, that became at times like the tawdry charm of a street urchin. I was disgusted with myself, and worried. I had thought I was above this kind of thing. I accused Raoul Cérusier of returning at an inconvenient moment. I found myself thinking that all the profound changes that I thought I could see in me might be no more than a pleasing illusion for which I could thank Renée. I was nothing but a easily beguiled lover, naively eager to see myself and make myself into the kind of man a woman wants to love, but shrewd and determined.

On the metro platform, where my wanderings had led me, I noticed the mirror on the coin-operated weighing scales. I fell to contemplating my face. My fears seemed horribly justified. I remembered seeing just these charmer's eyes with their teasing gaze in the faces of men eaten up with a wish to please that drives them to resort to all kinds of lies. I let a train go by. Nearby, people were noticing the excessive interest I seemed to have in my own image. I caught the fascinated eye of a metro employee reflected in the mirror, so to justify my presence on the scale, which he could have accused me of monopolising, I fed a coin into the machine's slot.

I realised that I had lost six or seven kilos, doubtless due to the anxiety and emotion of my metamorphosis. That fact did not just then seem significant. Another train drew in. Once I'd found a seat, I remembered the shed kilos and suddenly the idea flashed into my mind that not only had my head changed but perhaps so had my body and everything that went with it: arms, legs, heart, lungs, brain, toes, nervous system—in fact there was nothing left of Raoul Cérusier but my belief in his existence.

I stared at my hands. It seemed as if they had not changed. They were the same square, stubby-fingered hands. The left one still carried the scar I had shown to Julien Gauthier. I didn't want to rely on this one piece of evidence so I ate a hurried lunch and went home directly. Standing in front of the mirror, I noticed that my waist and shoulders seemed narrower, but since I'd lost six or seven kilos that was hardly surprising. I wasn't in the habit of examining my body in the mirror, or only in passing. I thought, however, that somewhere in the region of my navel I used to have a beauty spot which had now disappeared. Still, I couldn't be completely certain it had ever been there. I could be mixing it up with the navel of a friend or a relative. And besides, I was employing a good deal of will-power in maintaining my doubts on these points, reserving myself the option of adopting one or the other personality at my own convenience. I was still puzzling over this when Renée, the children safely sent off to school, joined me again. She was wearing a charming new dress and I couldn't help thinking that it must have cost her a pretty penny. I complimented her on it. She laughed, pleased, but, far from happy and holding me close, she murmured:

"I so wanted to be beautiful for you. I'm afraid, already I'm afraid. I feel as if you're only passing through, that you're not truly settled here, that you're full of uncertainty about yourself and everything around you. I'm wrong, aren't I?"

"Yes, dear Renée, quite wrong. I am what you might call the opposite of a restless man. I have such a stability of character and sentiments that I'm even a little ashamed of it at times. Of course, there is something different about me since I met you Renée, and it does affect my habits and way of life. It's true I'm a little restless these days, but my restlessness is purely a response to yours. I too am afraid. I would almost like to say that your life … "

She wouldn't let me finish. "Oh no!" she said three times, and began to cry bitterly. I entreated, "Dear heart, you mustn't cry." She wept all over my face and hands. I was overwhelmed; I felt like nothing more than a cheap looking glass, reflecting every thought and feeling that approached me. Darling, sweetheart, angel—these are the words I whispered to her.

"Roland, please forgive me, I've just been a little

unhappy. Since this evening. I called you, forgive me Roland, I called and you weren't there."

"What? It was you? Twice, wasn't it? The first time I thought I'd dreamt it. At the second, half-awake, I reached the telephone too late. My sweet child, God, if I had known. Of course I should have known, I should!"

"But you really mustn't think that I called you to make sure you were home at one in the morning. I swear it wasn't that. I was so unhappy, I needed to hear your voice. Oh Roland! I wanted to hear you say my name. This morning I wanted to cry, and then there was this letter."

"A letter? You alarm me."

"You mustn't be frightened, it's nothing. A letter from Bucharest, a pointless thing, four tedious pages with no news at all, but I felt a shadow fall over me, a threat. Oh, don't think that his return will stop us from seeing each other. It will make no difference to us, and when I speak of a threat I'm only thinking of myself, of his returning to my life, to every day of my life. If only you understood, if only you knew him. I would have liked to say nothing about him to you, but my heart is break-ing, I cannot stay silent. He is truly an odious, detestable creature. No, I'm exaggerating, that's not true. Neither odious nor detestable, nor even basically stupid, you have to recognise his good points too. But he's dull, that's what he is. Dull. And he has no idea of it. Besides, he's never aware of anything, never guesses how I feel. For him there is nothing but solid evidence, the most crudely built feelings. Everything that is beyond words is beyond him, and many other things are too. How have I found the strength and patience to live with such a mediocre man? Perhaps in the faint hope or vision meeting you. Roland?"

"That could be it, Renée. Yes that must be it. Women often have such premonitions—and men too, you know. Men too."

"My darling, you are handsome, you're refined and noble—you understand. I can say everything to you. With you, I don't hesitate, I talk, I weep, I talk again, I am yours, your Renée always. How strange it is. You are there, and I have to be clear and simple. And you don't know me, sad little housewife, stiff bourgeois lady, vain, greedy, someone's wife in fact! I'm like this because when I'm with him, I just have to keep my true self hidden. He is dull, so dull! He has a way of looking at everything as if it were for eating. At lunch, the day before he left for Bucharest, he was eating some sausage. He said, and he smacked his lips: "A good bit of sausage; there's nothing better." My God, I don't blame him for liking sausage and for saying it, even in that way. But why, each time he's on the point of opening his mouth, must I expect to hear something like that? The worst of it is, perhaps, that while he's dull and thick-skinned, nevertheless there is nothing in his behaviour that merits serious reproach. He's jovial and conscientious, a good father and a good husband. He does what he can to be pleasant with me, I couldn't say otherwise. And it is that which hurts me so deeply; since I'm suffering the attentions of an irreproachable man, whom can I blame for this if not myself? I can only accuse myself of my mistake, my humiliating, degrading mistake. A man can easily choose the wrong woman and live with her and suffer for it. He tolerates her. But living with a man she doesn't love, a woman suffers. That is what spoils her and nothing can repair it. I'm ashamed of him, I'm ashamed to death here before you, but I'm even more ashamed of myself, of my own mistake. Look at me, scorn me. I have spent years trying to make the best of my error and reconcile myself to it. I can hardly bear to admit to myself the hatred and remoteness which that man has always inspired in me. And yet I do hate him, I hate him."

"You mustn't exaggerate Renée."

"Yes, I know, mine is a very ordinary case, classic, that of a woman who believes she has wasted her life, who dreams of other possible fates, more worthy of her and more beautiful. I agree with you, it's quite comical. Perfect for superior types who like to sharpen their wit on easy targets. But if one is truly good, and indulgent, one is satisfied with a smile: one mustn't exaggerate."

Renée fell into another fit of crying. I felt less good, less sympathetic towards her than before. Still, I did my best to console her. No angel, but stern words, a somewhat pedantic way of analysing her case which soothed her misery. I understood her sadness, for it was mine too; I knew very well the kind of man she had to suffer. With a very bitter kind of delectation, I sketched out for her a good likeness of her man. All considered, the portrait showed a decent chap. Renée conceded this, but balanced it by dwelling on the absurdities of his character, which frankly became quite funny. I let go, laughing along with her. I really felt I had nothing left in common with this poor Cérusier.

Around half-past five, before going back to the fourth floor, Renée once more looked close to tears thinking of the next day, which was Sunday. The children would not be at school and would take up all her afternoon. A day without seeing me would be unbearable. Shyly, she suggested that she come to me once the maid had left, when the children would be in bed and asleep. At these words, my fatherly conscience rebelled and, suddenly entirely Cérusier, I was going to say, "Never, not on my life, to abandon your two children, anything could happen." But:

"If you like, Renée my darling, I will come downstairs to you."

She recoiled at first, shocked, then accepted with shining eyes. The prospect of secretly gaining access to my home sent shivers across my scalp and the rest of my body.

Once Renée had left, I began to sort through my business correspondence, which kept me busy in the flat until evening. It was half-past eight when I went out to Manière's. The Sarrazine, to whom I had not given a thought for the last week, was there with friends. Seeing me come in, she gave a pretty, joyful smile, to which I responded by smiling discreetly, almost distractedly. Finding her here disturbed me. I had focused everything on Renée and the drama of being once more in my home with her, though in the guise of a stranger, and now the reappearance of the Sarrazine, who did mean something to me, cut across and muddied these emotions. The conversation at her table was animated. She joined in, not looking at me, with such spirit and liveliness that I was almost jealous of her. She looked even more beautiful to me than that first evening, sat in exactly the same seat as before. Her lovely face with its slightly masculine lines appeared to me as if touched with a gentler light, and her stony eyes also had a softer sheen. She was wearing a dress of thick woollen fabric, a rich midnight blue, with steel buttons rising in a line right up to her chin and forming a curve over her bust which rose and fell as she breathed. I've often thought since that one of the Sarrazine's charms was her air of modesty, which seemed a natural property of her body rather than the result of careful effort.

I was just beginning my supper when she came over to my table and sat down facing me. Chin resting on the back of her hand, her eyes on mine, she said a little hoarsely:

"Here you are again. You left me very abruptly the night we met. I was angry. I didn't want to see you again. I didn't go to our rendezvous the next day, and then I went away and while I was travelling I thought of you. I was happy, but also afraid of never finding you again. Have you been waiting for me too? Have you been thinking of me?"

"Sarrazine, you are so beautiful."

"Do you see that dark-haired young lady, at my table, facing you? One evening, at midnight, I went to her bedroom to tell her. I told her that I was the Sarrazine,

127

that I was in love with you. I spoke of you as if we were engaged. I didn't have your address but I wrote you letters that I tore up, a sixteen-year-old's letters. I feel different. Anna said I look younger. Is it true? You say nothing. I came back from my voyage yesterday. I leave again this evening, yes, almost at once, for five days. I will be back on Thursday evening at the latest. Will you meet me Thursday evening? At eight? Where? OK, at the Junot. I love you."

X

I LOOKED FORWARD TO the week's respite entailed by the Sarrazine's absence, almost relieved at the thought. During our brief conversation she had said she would have two hours free between the end of her supper and her train's departure. I could have asked her to spend those two hours with me. I knew she would not refuse, but I said nothing. As she left me to rejoin her friends, she leant over my table and said softly, "Your joy is well-hidden, but I shall not let that frighten me. On my journey I shall remember your reserved air and I'll reassure myself by thinking that for you our meeting is a very serious thing." Truthfully, this affair did not yet seem so important, but I knew that one day soon it would really begin. No longer bound to a wife to make me blush when I lied, there was no doubt I would let myself be tamed by my Sarrazine. I felt all the more helpless since I had good reason to try to forget Renée and the children. Yet I was in no hurry to let her claws close on me. Without actually thinking of missing our rendezvous, I hoped vaguely for some new reprieve.

Besides, my mind was full of another meeting—with Renée the following evening. All Sunday I couldn't stop thinking about it. Disappointment caught up with me at the last minute. Back at home that evening I found a letter from Renée under my door, informing me that one of her cousins from Blois was spending a few days in Paris and had decided to stay with her. We had always welcomed her warmly before and it was out of the question to send her to a hotel now. Over the next few days, Renée struggled to find any free time. Cousin Janette loved her like a daughter and would hardly leave her alone. I called Uncle Antonin to ask him to visit Renée and take her to Chatou for twenty-four hours at least, but his car was, as he explained, in a transitional period and he hadn't the heart to go far from the piggery while the engine, wheels and bodywork, so quartered and scattered, demanded all his care and attention. Distracted as he was, he could scarcely attend to my problems as well.

I received a note to say that on Tuesday afternoon, while accompanying her cousin to shop at the Bon-Marché, Renée would see to it that she lost herself in the crowd and would meet me in a café on the Rue de Sèvres. It was past five when she stepped into the café. She had had much ado getting round cousin Janette's affectionate vigilance, being found twice in the crowd before managing to escape. The wait had seemed long, my good humour was wearing thin and I wasn't overjoyed to see that she had bought herself a new leopard-trimmed coat. The year before I had had the greatest trouble in making her accept one of astrakhan, the cost of which had seemed to her a pointless folly. In the end she had resigned herself reluctantly to picking out a cheaper one. It had probably cost less than this three-quarter-length leopard thing, which looked like the highest quality. She was very elegant but I didn't say a word, though I was pleased to see the interest generated by her entrance among the groups seated around us in the café. I listened rather coldly to her complaints about cousin Janette.

"It's late," I observed after a moment. "Let's walk somewhere, if you like."

We walked in silence down the Rue de Sèvres, Renée troubled by my coolness, and I likewise. She looked up at me with eyes I guessed were anxious, but I pretended to look elsewhere. On the Rue du Dragon, she took my arm and asked shyly, with a slight tremble in her voice:

"Roland, have I vexed you? I'm sorry."

"No, I'm not vexed. Why should you think me vexed?"

Renée did not reply, disconcerted and hurt by this refusal to yield to her. The street was gloomy, almost deserted. A foolish pride stopped me from taking her in my arms and lifting her from her despondency. I felt her hand shaking on my arm. Our walk went on for a few minutes in a miserable silence. We were just coming up to a bus stop on the Boulevard Saint-Germain when Renée, gripping my hand in hers, looked up at me, her face transformed with fear.

"Roland," she asked, "it isn't over for us?"

"Renée what are you thinking? I have been stupid— and unfair. Punish me, but don't be afraid any more. When you have made someone close to you suffer and when you have seen such anguish in her eyes, you really do have to love her as long as you live."

The lines of her face relaxed. She kissed my sleeve and, leaning her head on my shoulder, smiled with delight. Passengers stepping down from their bus at the stop watched this charming, joyful scene, and among them, just as we drew level with him, was Julien Gauthier. I am sure he recognised me. His hard, determined gaze was fixed on mine. The encounter shook me somewhat. It risked reviving the dangerous suspicion Julien had formed on listening to my confession. My intimacy with Renée and our carelessness in parading it through the city might not only make an enemy of him but could even imply that we now had nothing to fear from Renée's husband. It was a short step from there to imagining that I had actually done away with the spouse myself. Knowing me to be Renée's lover, he might now see my madness in a very different light. He might very well read my reckless meanderings as proof of criminal intent. These reflections took no more than a few seconds. Renée had seen nothing and didn't even know where she was. I hurried her on, but Julien Gauthier overtook us and, perhaps wondering whether he had really seen Raoul Cérusier's wife on my arm, turned openly to stare at us, his expression both menacing and anxious. He appeared about to address Renée and I think all that stopped him was the fundamental antipathy he had always felt for her. She recognised him. Dropping my arm in fright, she hissed: "One of my husband's friends. Did you see how he stared at us? How rude. But I was always rather cool with him and this is his revenge." Indeed she had always shown him, as with all my friends from before our marriage, a decided hostility, perhaps sensing the threat of these long-held bonds which can awaken old, free-thinking habits in the most docile of husbands. Besides, Julien had never made an effort to overcome her resistance, for my wife had irritated him visibly ever since the earliest days of our marriage, and they quickly came to detest each other. I found out later that it was this that stopped him from going to find her the day I thought I had confided my secret to him.

I was rather surprised by Renée's manner and by her discomfort at this encounter. From the few words she spoke, I understood that she was horribly afraid of Julien's committing some indiscretion. And yet, only five minutes ago, she had agreed with apparent indifference to undermine her own household for the sake of a reassuring word from my lips. I told myself that she was torn between her roles of wife and lover, as indeed was I by my double identity, and concluded that everything my metamorphosis had shown me could be discovered by any man in the same situation. All this time, Julien was walking a few paces ahead of us down the Rue des Saints-Pères, where I was following him, to show I had nothing to fear. He looked back from time to time and, seeing us walking side by side and preserving a proper distance between us, he might have thought that our abandon just a moment ago was no more than an instant's illusion. Increasingly anxious, Renée began to interrogate me.

"Why did we have to follow him?" she demanded. "It's ridiculous, one would think you were going out of your way to provoke him."

I began to explain my intention. She wouldn't let me speak.

"Of course, you heed nothing but your own fantasy;

133

you don't care a jot for the consequences this encounter might have. You're a free man but I have a husband; I have children. There's no need for you to care about that, but it's my whole life."

"Don't lose your temper here Renée. He could hear you and think we're having a lovers' quarrel."

At which I gave a dry chuckle, as they do in the theatre to underline a stinging retort. Entirely caught up in her own fears and bitter humour, Renée didn't notice. We turned into Rue Jacob and, Julien being safely out of sight, she said to me with a sweet smile, "Darling, I've been horrid." I replied, "You haven't at all, only you've no pretence about you, that's all." "Oh Roland, you just won't let yourself understand." "But I do, truly, so well!" And so on, right through till half-past six. But for me, the true drama began around nine that evening, in the solitude of my apartment, as I wondered just what Julien Gauthier might do. If he chose to speak to the police, I was lost. Of course, it could not be proved that I had done away with Cérusier and I decided that, if need be, I would deny everything I had confessed to Julien. But I had no status in the eyes of the authorities, and no way of answering their charges. The false papers I had thought of obtaining would do nothing for me in such a situation. I reassured myself, remembering that Julien believed he had proof of his friend's departure for Bucharest. He must be afraid that Cérusier would find himself in mortal danger on his return, and perhaps this evening he might be sure of that—still, nothing yet confirmed that the crime was already accomplished. I could reasonably suppose that he'd restrict himself to watching for Raoul's return in order to warn him as quickly as possible. Perhaps he would even write to him. In any case, even if he did tip off the police, he would hardly dare to supplement what was mere suspicion by reporting Renée's infidelity as well. He would have to make do with reporting our conversation in the café and giving them a fairly vague description of my appearance. The police would investigate my home and office, they'd telephone the Romanian consulate where I'd already taken care to have my passport stamped and, reassured, they would close my case. Cérusier's absence then continuing for an unusually long period, they would eventually have to reopen the file, but between now and then I would have time to make my own precautions.

I slept very badly. Part of my night was spent imagining my arrest and, over and over, my cross-examination. "Right," the superintendent would say, "you were born in X … on 1st June 1900. Good. Your parents both practised the profession of watchmaker in that village. Is that correct?"

"Yes, superintendent."

"You are lying again. Neither in X, nor in Y, nor in Z are you mentioned in the civil records. And now, I've had enough of your lies. Sergeant Lefort, work on that man until he's willing to tell us his true identity."

"Superintendent sir, I'll tell you everything. I've had a metamorphosis."

135

"A metamorphosis? How very interesting. I've always been fascinated by metamorphoses."

"Yes, one day, all of a sudden, my face changed. It became another man's face. I couldn't claim to be Raoul Cérusier any more; I had to change my name too."

"How curious. Sergeant, come here, in case our young friend requires our help. So your face was changed. You must have been very unhappy."

"Absolutely, superintendent sir. You can imagine my distress."

"Calm down, my boy, your troubles are over now. We will look after you very well. Indeed I know of an establishment where the doctors specialise in metamorphoses."

"No, let me go! I don't want that! Let go of me! I want to go! No, no, no!"

"Sergeant, the straitjacket."

When I awoke from that dreadful night, I was in a state of such nervousness that no doubt it contributed to my strange behaviour with Lucienne the next morning. Work now gave me a reason, or at least a pretext, to go to the office every day. As I walked in, and generally when I was thinking objectively about it, I was determined to maintain with Lucienne the kind of manner that would restore myself in her opinion. Yet, when she was there, my wish to please her won out and I returned despite myself to those little tricks I used to mark myself as a particular protégé. This wish to please was understandable, to an extent. It was also a wish to restore this woman's love for me, and her friendship too. I wanted, deeply, to be protected from complete isolation. And there was in this lovely, honest girl, with her warm bright eyes, a strength and a gentleness which seemed to signal safety to me, and it was as if by holding her in my arms I could take refuge there. However, her reserved manner verged increasingly on contempt and scarcely encouraged me to confide in her. I was in danger of telling her, with brimming eyes, my God you are so lovely; or, instead, as we read the same document together, I would lean my head against hers or even, under the table, my knee against her knee. Each time this happened, she would briskly lead us back to the subject at hand, and with such curt words that I was always humiliated.

That morning, I didn't see Mme Lagorge at her window. I asked, "Isn't Mme Lagorge in today?" "She had someone call in for her just now, to say she was unwell," replied Lucienne. I was excited to think we were alone together. I thought of making my confession there and then, and loudly; I pictured passionate protests, an organ blast sweeping away all objections. It was a moment of private fancy. Aloud, I explained to Lucienne, quite calmly, precisely what business brought me to the office today. It was to do with a client hesitating over a deal, with whom we would need to agree prices a little lower than usual. Only Lucienne was in a position to decide. We exchanged opinions on the issue. We were standing in the middle of my study. I was arguing the importance of the deal, half-heartedly, too engrossed in Lucienne, in her open, serious expression, her tall athletic body with its adolescent air. She tried to recall a precedent to establish her decision and she screwed up her mouth and frowned with the effort of the thought. Watching her, I felt tenderness flood my body. Taking her head in both my hands, I pressed my lips to her forehead and murmured fervent words. She pushed me away abruptly, her eyes flaming with fury, and said in her most controlled voice:

"You are an idiot, an utter idiot."

"Lucienne, I love you. I beg you, listen to me. I'm asking you to marry me."

"That's impossible."

"Lucienne, try to understand me. You're angry. I know I'm awkward, I make everyone hate me. Don't say it's impossible. Don't answer lightly or in the heat of your anger. You are my whole life."

"I'm answering you, this time without anger: it's impossible."

The tone was clear. There was nothing more to say, but I was full of grand feelings and my love seemed very beautiful to me. I could not allow myself to be cut off when I'd only just begun. I wanted at least to engage in a heart-rending argument, which would give some substance to my defeat. Taking advantage of Mme Lagorge's absence, I began to proclaim that my life was ruined, that I had been dreadfully foolish to believe that fate would change her mind. Consigned to the misery of a solitude that would embrace all the peculiar monsters of my sort, that's what I was. I who was generally so happy to be alive—I cursed the hour of my birth. Lucienne said nothing. In the hope of clinching the question, I reproached her for playing with my affections, for doing everything to encourage my feelings for her while she meant to rebuff me all along. Exasperated, she moved towards the door.

"Do I disgust you?"

"Yes, a little," she said, before disappearing into the other room.

Lucienne's contemptuous tone as she pronounced these words infuriated me. At this point, my night of anguish and delirium began to make its effects felt. A brutish anger rushed to my head like alcohol, though still leaving me with enough sense to understand the ignominy of my conduct. I threw myself after her, almost tearing down the door in my fervour. Lucienne was sitting on the table, with one leg dangling, her head turned towards the window. I approached her and said, this time without shouting but in a voice thick with rage:

"So I disgust you, do I? And Cérusier, he doesn't disgust you at all? You really do like him, don't you? He told me everything, at Bourget's. Two weeks it went on. He described everything. One day, just like today, Lagorge wasn't in. You had spent the morning in his office filing papers and he embraced you several times. At noon, he whispered to you: 'I'm going to lock the main door.' You went quite pink with emotion, with happiness. I'm telling you, he told me everything."

At first Lucienne had stared at me in alarm, then her face hardened and I began to think she might strike me, but she turned away, towards the window. I saw her eyelashes flutter and her jaw clench in the effort of hold-ing back her tears. My presence no longer offended her and my words no longer reached her in her pride. She was utterly broken, wounded to the depths of her soul. I saw it, but I wanted to make her tears flow. I was wait-ing for this piece of proof with a grim jealousy, which merged somehow with another feeling, something like gratitude and admiration. But the passionate urge to destroy, to defile, carried me on.

"I tell you, he wouldn't leave anything to the imagina-tion. His business trip to Nancy, on which you accompa-nied him during your so-called illness, for all that Mme Lagorge knows; the two days you spent together there; the two nights. Apparently you wore a pair of white silk pyjamas that were a rapture to behold. 'Old man,' Cérusier said to me—you know how he is, a bit vulgar— 'old man, you'd have thought she was a snow princess.' Oh, I won't repeat everything he told me, for instance about a certain pair of stockings, on the first morning in Nancy, or about a certain afternoon taxi ride. I couldn't do it. I'm not lucky enough to know how to make women love me. I'm nothing but a boor, an unlucky type, yet there are still some things I would not do. Well, I assure you, there's nothing Cérusier wouldn't do. I was ashamed for him, and sorry for you before I knew you. What a revelation. And yet, I'm only a distant acquaintance, out of touch for the last ten years. Ah! You really don't know him at all."

She was weeping, her head erect, eyes wide open. The tears flowed down her cheeks and dripped onto the starched white collar of her blouse, where they made little wet puffs.

"He went as far as recounting, about you, that first word after love-making, so touching, you know: 'Your eyes … ' "

Lucienne gave a sob, then a moan that was barely audible, the moan of a little girl who has been hurt. I saw her large hand dangling open there, as if it had nothing more to hold and had let go of life. And suddenly, it seemed as if my heart cracked in two. I fell to my knees and begged her to forgive me.

"You mustn't believe me. Raoul said never said anything like that. I swear it. One day, I'll tell you. I'll write down how I knew, but you must understand that Raoul never told me anything. Oh Lucienne! You don't believe me now, you can't believe me, and yet only now am I telling the truth."

"Go away," Lucienne murmured. "Leave me alone."

I stood up and backed out of the room as softly as I could. I was in despair and so horrified at my behaviour and myself that there in the street I began to run as if I could escape the hideous beast that had just reared up in me, and leave it far behind. In my flight, I hurtled into a kind of muscleman in a thick sweater, who grasped my arm with one hand and forced me to turn and face him, saying: "Hey, Mr Artist, show some manners." Paying no attention to the way I went, still running, I found myself heading back the way I'd come and eventually stopped in front of my office building. A thought had just struck me and I froze in fear. I had left Lucienne in such a state

141

of desperation and forced her to abandon such a full and intimate affection that I thought her natural sense of balance could hardly resist and she might well kill herself. I wanted to go to her, but didn't dare. Shame, and also the fear that my odious presence might only confirm her terrible resolve, pinned me to the spot. My trouble must have been visible, for the sturdy gentleman whom I'd jostled a moment ago, just passing me now in the street, spoke again, this time with some sympathy in his voice. "Monsieur has some problem?" he offered, not expecting a reply. After several minutes' hesitation, I decided to call Lucienne by telephone from Bucharest.

"Hello, is that Mme Lagorge?"

"No," said a voice so choked up that it was barely recognisable.

"Is that Lucienne? Cérusier here. I'm calling from Bucharest, just back from a stay in Sofia. Is everything OK?"

"Yes. Thank you."

"Nothing new at the office? Business going well? And the new boy, is he getting some work done?"

"Yes, he's working."

"Lucienne, your voice does sound odd. One might think you were angry. I called really because I wanted to talk to you, to be with you."

I heard a sob down the line, then a kind of mumble.

"Lucienne, you're crying."

"Me? No. But speaking of your friend, M Colbert came by just now to ask me if he could, exceptionally, accept a lower price from a new client."

She explained the offer to me in detail, and I managed to draw her into a conversation about the business. Lucienne seemed to forget her distress and her tone picked up. I ended by saying:

"I value you so highly that I ought really to bow to your opinion. Do as you think best, then. But swear that you won't forget me."

"Goodness," she sighed "I'm happy to promise that."

That sigh, which sounded infinitely tender to me, served to conclude our conversation, for I cut the call short on purpose. I would scarcely have been able to bear hearing her say that she loved me still and in spite of everything. Besides, nothing led me to believe that she would have said that; the tone of her words could easily have been interpreted as meaning something entirely different. But ever since seducing my wife, I felt oddly intuitive, especially on questions of the heart.

That afternoon, having business in town, I could not stop myself from loitering near the office. I was obsessed with the pathetic scene I had made that morning, although I no longer feared for Lucienne. Three times I walked past the door of the building without the least desire to go in, with no intention other than to appease my obsession. The absurdity of my game began to annoy me and I was about to make for the opposite pavement when I saw in the middle of the street, standing by himself on a traffic island, Julien Gauthier, waiting for the right moment to cross. His presence in the area, only a day after he'd seen me out with Renée, made me nervous. He often used to drop in at the office and he knew Lucienne, whom he

found quite charming. He would naturally think of pro-
posing they work together on some strategy to stop the
madman. Indeed, just then I saw him enter the building
then step into the lift, and while the lift was making its
slow ascent, I was able to enter in my turn and, looking
up from the ground floor, make sure—without being
seen—that he stepped out again at the third floor.

XI

SUMMONED BY TELEPHONE, Uncle Antonin was to meet me that same evening in a café on the Boulevard de Clichy that he'd already pointed out to me. I was there at half-past nine, and since he hadn't arrived yet I decided to stroll outside in the street for at least a little while. In my nervous state I would have found the wait indoors very difficult. It was cold and damp; the fog made haloes around the electric street lamps. I wandered back and forth on the side of the street that loses its daytime animation at this hour, having little to whet the curiosity of night-walkers. I had gone barely fifty paces to a street corner when a girl spoke to me: "Say, pet, come see how sweet I am." Her soft drawl reminded me of my native province. She was very young and her slender waist, her slight frame, made her appear even younger. She must be new to the profession, a little housemaid whom the street had stolen from her kitchen. She seized my sleeve, and I saw her hand, tiny, but red and swollen, which she hadn't the time to care for. I stopped to gaze at her pretty, childishly artful face. It seemed as if the little maid was offering me a way to escape my struggle with my own perilous situation. I was overcome with a desire to follow her, or rather to flee with her far from Paris and to attach my life and my cares to this fragile thread of hope. Only the most serious and devoted of men feel this sudden feverish desire to toss the dice on such slim odds, counting on a lucky chance that would never befall them in the ordinary course of a harsh and complicated existence.

"Well, pretty boy?"

"It's cold," I said. "What filthy weather, what a filthy life. Tell me, wouldn't you like to forget all of this a while and see other countries with sunshine and everything that's lacking here? We could go by train, perhaps a ship … "

"Stay a moment," interrupted the little maid. "Don't worry. I understand, you know, but I don't work for the white slave trade."

She gave a little laugh of commiseration and her eyes shone with pride and pleasure.

"You won't believe me, but the profession I'm following now is just a temporary thing. Take a good look at me and remember my face. In two months and maybe sooner I'll be in the movies. Because, you see, my friend works in cinema."

Curious to learn more, I offered to buy her a hot toddy. She chattered as we walked along.

"As I told you, this job is just for the mean time. But it's also to prepare me, because of the atmosphere. Victor wants me to play realist parts. I'd rather be the parlour-boarder type, girl about town, but realist is good too. As Victor says, everyone has their own particular gift. With me it's realist, he saw that straight away. He's working on a film for me right now. We'll shoot the outdoors parts on the Côte d'Azur, or in Argentina, he's still deciding. The best thing for me is that there'll be a part for my sister Léonie too. We're going to bring her down from the country one of these days soon."

I let her steer me towards her chosen café. We were still following the street I had been strolling on. A delivery van heading towards us stopped right there, beside us. I seized the little maid by the arm and, leaning close in to her so she would hear me above the sound of the engine, I exclaimed:

"But that's ridiculous! You can't seriously believe in this cock-and-bull story about the movies. It's a pack of lies. Don't you see that your Victor is a crook?"

"Hold on a second. I know there are guys who try to catch girls like that. Victor told me about them. But wait a moment. Victor's already done a test shoot with me. And I saw myself on a screen. Yes, on a screen, I saw it myself. It's amazing. On the screen."

Just then, a hand came down onto my shoulder and I was pulled backwards. Thinking it must be Victor, I turned round, ready to defend myself. It was Uncle Antonin, looking at me in a way that worried me at once. At the sight of this man with his long moustache, whom she no doubt believed to be a cop, the little maid took to her heels and, darting across the avenue, was lost in the crowd in seconds. The uncle stared fixedly at me, not hiding his contempt. Perceiving my evident surprise at his expression, he eventually deigned to say cuttingly:

"Blackguard. You really thought you were running rings round me with your stories of metamorphoses and such-like. And I fell for it, like a lamb. How stupid I have been. I do kick myself."

"But what's the matter, Uncle? What has made you change your mind all of a sudden?"

"Everything now makes me believe it, everything. Wretch. And yet I would still be taken in by your lies if I hadn't caught you chasing a tart. But I saw you. I saw you."

"I don't understand. What link do you see between my chasing a tart, as you put it, and my identity?"

"What link? Ah, my boy! You think yourself so clever and indeed you are, but you haven't thought of everything. Or perhaps, you don't know my nephew very well. Understand that Raoul is a serious man, a man who knows his duty—I mean he's a man. Raoul would never use a second of his spare time to go hanging off the arm of a street girl as I've just seen you doing. No, never."

"This on top of everything! Raoul was serious but he also had his moments of weakness. But now you're making me talk about him in the third person. This is crazy!"

"Ah, ah! I've got you now!"

"Uncle, I beg you. Look at me. No, don't look at me but listen, listen to your nephew's voice. A false friend could be mistaken, but you? You don't believe me. Allow me at least to tell you how these things happened. I was walking up and down outside, waiting for you. A girl accosts me." I told him the story of the little maid, which he heard out without a word.

"When you appeared, I was trying to make her see her own naivety. I had taken her arm in a movement of pity, and of anger too, wanting almost to shake her and give more weight to my words."

"The poor child," said Uncle Antonin. "It's monstrous. We could try to find her again."

"It will be impossible, and probably useless. So Uncle, do you still hold to your belief that I'm a scoundrel and an impostor?"

"No, of course not. I ask only to believe that you are my nephew."

His reply was both evasive and hesitant, although perhaps unintentionally. What was more, he continued to address me formally rather than as family, as he always had before. I was almost certain he wouldn't do this on purpose—which was hardly reassuring all the same. Eventually, we went back to the café where we'd intended to meet. Passing the van which had brought him, Uncle explained that his old car was not in a driveable state at the moment and he described the main transformations he was trying out on her. He was still talking about it when we sat down. Somehow this had won back his trust, as if analysing his car's metamorphosis allowed him to understand the technicalities of mine. He began to call me nephew again.

"And now?" he asked. "What is wrong? You worried me when you called."

"My situation has become more complicated, maybe even dangerous now. I have reason to believe that Julien Gauthier has stepped in."

At the name Julien Gauthier, which evoked a very particular attitude to my adventure, the uncle's face darkened and he seemed to be trying hard to suppress a doubt that remained at the back of his mind. His entire expression changed. I went on, in spite of this:

"This is what's happened. Yesterday evening, around

149

six o'clock, I was out walking with Renée, and Julien came across us. He turned to look, and walked ahead of us to make sure he was right. He was even more surprised because we were walking arm-in-arm. For him, everything was clear. He didn't say a word to us, didn't even greet us, but he didn't hesitate to look us up and down, just as you might examine criminals who ought to account for their actions. He must be thinking I'm taking up a deuced lot of space in his friend Raoul's life; perhaps I'm taking up all of it."

"Naturally," Uncle responded in spite of himself, as if struck by my idea.

"Why do you say naturally?"

"I say naturally because it's natural."

In asking this I had given in to an impulse of anger. He replied in a tone of defiance. And added: "I've a right to my opinion." I thought I had better stop there with my confessions. There was a moment of painful silence between us. I saw in front of me the only person who could be my witness begin to detach himself from the truth of the two aspects of my fate. If he denied me his understanding, refused to bear witness for me, I could end up believing that my whole adventure was no more than the meandering of an over-strained imagination. I felt as if I were assisting at a man's deathbed. Uncle too was troubled and watched me anxiously. Doubts crowded into his face; the absurdity of such a metamorphosis appeared to him increasingly clear and he only continued to hesitate out of a sense of fidelity to his position. However, there remained in my favour the links of friendship and complicity that had been forged between us, and above all his horror at such an inescapable dilemma—for he had to be with me or against me, to decide if I was a crook or a victim. He had been able to make this difficult choice just a moment ago, in the heat of his anger. A misleading incident had forced him to. Now, thinking coolly and with time to reflect, he hesitated to choose his side. I thought I saw a way to reassert my case.

"Uncle, let's speak frankly. You still have doubts—more than doubts. I'm going to ask you the question I would have asked Julien if we'd taken the conversation further. If I were not Raoul Cérusier, why in hell's name would I have confessed such things to you? It's an enormous risk for me. Did I need your help to become Renée's lover? No. Have I tried to extort money from you? I could have taken advantage of your trust and generosity, for you did offer to help me financially. Did I do it? You might also imagine that I wanted to be sure of your support and to use your authority in persuading Renée that I was her husband. But each time you offered to step in to help me, I have categorically refused. Remember, one evening at Chatou, I was even angry at your offer. It's no good, whichever way I try to look at it. Apart from the truth, I really see no other explanation for my behaviour. Have you any ideas?"

"I? What do you think? None at all."

"Naturally, you might still think I'm mad. Julien's convinced of that and he has his own logic, since my claim that I've changed faces is enough to prove my madness

151

for him. In any case, you have no more reason to think me mad than you did yesterday or three weeks ago. Having seen me walking with a little tart off the street, you cried impostor. That's taking things a little quickly, but it happens to everyone—deciding on a moment's impulse—and that's not the crux of the argument, since after all you have agreed that my intentions were pure. At the very least, I hope you no longer doubt me on that point."

"No, no doubt on that one. That would be ridiculous. And even if your intentions had not been pure, I recognise now that the assumption was somewhat unfounded."

"So?"

"Yes, of course. I agree there isn't a single new reason to justify my fears."

Uncle Antonin fell silent and, gazing distractedly at my tie, he began to pull at the tips of his moustache. I waited for the result of his meditation, my heart thumping. Eventually he muttered, without raising his eyes and in a regretful tone, as if he'd fought off his own convictions:

"All the same, Raoul, all the same. To change one's face like that, all at once, is not natural. It's not something that can be allowed by a man of sound reason."

My last hope had vanished. Belief in the absurd is a state of grace which one attains as if by a magical charm. Once the spell is broken, for whatever reason, no effort of argument or persuasion can restore belief. Uncle must have realised that this particular grace had left him and I had an idea he felt himself diminished, impoverished.

He stole a glance at me, nervy as a deserter, and I believe he was aware and ashamed of betraying the cause of the Absurd. In any case, he hadn't the will to clarify his position. He began several times to speak about Julien Gauthier, and I realised that he had decided he should meet him. Having made him admit it, I offered to engineer a meeting between the two of them. Uncle accepted gratefully.

"Perhaps this is a mistake," I sighed, "but never mind. At least I shall be present to defend myself. I cannot wait for this question to be settled once and for all. I don't expect you to appreciate my reasons, but maybe you will hear them with an open mind. That's all I can hope for."

Uncle protested, in all sincerity, that for him it was about nothing more than reassuring his conscience. We parted, having agreed a rendezvous for the day after next at midday in a restaurant near the Place de l'Étoile. I said that I would tell Julien.

There was no question for me that I should attend that luncheon. I had only taken charge in order to gain some breathing space, fearing that otherwise Uncle would speak to Julien Gauthier the very next day and give him information which Gauthier would not hesitate to turn to good use. There wasn't a shadow of doubt that my liberty was under threat. Julien's fears would have been confirmed by his discussion with Lucienne earlier that afternoon, for she could hardly have failed to recognise me in his portrait of the dangerous maniac who claimed to be Raoul Cérusier. This new revelation would seem significant. Not only had I taken his friend's place beside his wife, but I was also manoeuvring in such a way as to supplant him in his work. The question must have arisen of whether they ought to inform the police. Luckily, Julien still believed I was in Romania. The letters stamped from Bucharest testified to that. Nor was it impossible that he'd detected my ruse, especially if Lucienne realised that she had not once managed to see my face directly on the day of my departure. But it was unlikely she would remember this. Just like Mme Lagorge, she was surely convinced that she had seen me.

In any case, Julien did not have my address. The one I had given to Lucienne was invented and, even if this were already discovered, it would take a good two days to trace me back to Rue Caulaincourt. I would have liked to move out the very next morning, but I did not feel able to leave the neighbourhood, and perhaps Paris altogether, without seeing Renée once more, for I nursed a vain hope of taking her and the children with me. Her cousin was due to return to Blois tomorrow afternoon and we had already agreed to meet later that evening. Renée was to expect me at her apartment after nine o'clock, once the children were asleep. That same Thursday evening, the Sarrazine would also be expecting me at Café Junot, but I had sacrificed that encounter for one with my wife without hesitation, if not without regret.

I walked home via the lofty streets of Montmartre so I would come to the junction from Rue Girardon's sheltered incline, for I had a notion that Julien, realising the address I'd given to Lucienne was false, might have posted himself by my wife's home in the hope of picking up my trail again. Luckily, Rue Caulaincourt was deserted. On the fourth floor of my building, at the far end of the balcony, I observed that our bedroom window was brightly lit, all the shutters open. It was eleven in the evening. I found Renée waiting for me on the fifth-floor landing.

"I was on the balcony, I saw you coming."

"Your cousin?"

"At the cinema. We reserved our seats this afternoon and then, at the last minute, I had a terrible headache. Janette went with the maid. But you're home very late. My headache has hardly bought us much time."

"If only I'd known."

We entered my place, my bachelor's apartment. I was badly affected by Uncle Antonin's desertion. I listened distractedly to my wife, thinking that until now I had effectively concealed the consequences of my metamorphosis from myself, and that all the witnesses of my former life would leave me and I would be utterly alone. I sighed, like an old man.

"What's wrong?"

"Nothing," I said, sighing again. "If I had known I would see you this evening, I would have been ready to talk to you. Today, I thought of a number of thorny questions relating to you, and now I'm finding it hard to put them in order. I would like to ask you some of them, but with enough skill and severity that you will have to answer yes or no. If you reply: 'I don't know,' I'll have the right to interpret."

"Roland, I already know where your questions will lead: to making me confront my contradictions. If you wish to be fair, ask me nothing. I am giving you everything I can offer you. The contradictions you see are part of our proprieties. Besides, you understood that before I did."

The start of this discussion was quite indicative of what was to follow. My wife had not changed. I admired the way she suddenly returned to her cool-headed perspective as wife and matron. Her clear eyes told me: I love you, but that's not my whole life. I thought it pointless to push her further. My fate was adapting to my new look. Lucienne and Uncle Antonin had left me. My wife was preparing to do likewise. "What are you thinking?" Renée asked.

"I can't tell you, you just forbade me to. Did your cousin enjoy her stay in Paris?"

"Oh, go on, ask your questions, young man. Does 'young man' make you laugh? What can I do? I'm closer to thirty-five years old than the thirty I confessed to you. I have a family. And you, why you're a charming young man who came to Paris only three weeks ago with an allowance from your parents whom you left at home on a whim. Perhaps they hoped to stop you marrying a little shop assistant and when you talked of coming to Paris alone, like a man, they thought: 'And why not? He'll surely forget her.' You'll never know if your parents set you on this path or you chose it yourself. Things happened so quickly that you hadn't time to take your pressed flowers, nor your butterfly collection, nor your little shop girl. And when you made it to Paris, you became a naturalist and you seduced a married woman. That's about the measure of what happened. I'm not far wrong about the main elements. For the rest, I don't particularly wish for more detail. My darling, I wished so to overlook, to forget all that separates us and does not favour me. I should have realised that love alone would not satisfy you for long. You want to know everything, to have everything, and what you believe in most of all is the very thing most likely to unsettle and cool our love, and so I leave it in shadow, unexamined. I told you my husband is on the whole a dull man, an ordinary man, whom I accept reluctantly as my partner. That was sweet, don't you think? To tell your lover he is the light in your life and timidly to conceal from him that you are like all the rest, that you and your husband lead a life of cares, of shared trials, but of course that *is* sweet. As a well-brought-up young man, you ought to play along and not miss a moment when you might give me a hand with keeping up appearances. Instead of which, you're annoyed because you think you've seen the looming shadow of my husband while the poor man is still far off in Bucharest. You allow me nothing, neither my cousin Janette nor Raoul. For I've hidden that from you too—he has a Christian name. He's called Raoul. Since yesterday, you've looked at me as if you see betrayal in my eyes. Well, so be it. Ask me your questions or rather your question. You won't now? But do, ask me: 'In God's name, ultimately, yes or no, do you love him?' "

I couldn't help smiling, not because the situation was at all funny, but because Renée was superb.

157

"You are right—except for my being well and truly thirty-eight years old—I am not a young man but a child. I really was going to ask you some foolish questions. Yet the most important of them was not, as you suggest, to know whether you love him. More than anything I wanted to ask you whether you are ready to follow me to the other side of the earth. I shall ask no such thing now, but you must admit that this type of question has never spoilt any romantic novel. I might even have been able to say some rather pretty lines."

"I'm sure of it, Roland, and I would love to think about it. But I cannot pretend to you that I haven't just made new jams and that we must think about when to eat them. At the moment I'm knitting a little jumper for Toinette and I'm planning to go on to waistcoats, socks and slippers. What good to me is the other side of the world? I can make no longer journey than up these stairs to see you. Do my words hurt you?"

"No, on the contrary. I admire your wisdom. It's as if we've been married for many years and that I've managed to forget it just for three weeks. Are you sure it's really your husband who's in Bucharest?"

Considering my condition as one who has been transformed, this lovers' game seemed suddenly stupid and tedious. As Renée was just asking if I myself was sure of my little shop girl's whereabouts, I cut her short.

"Enough of this nonsense. There is no shop girl, nor any of the scenes you imagine. Here, there is a man who loves you, God knows why, and who could support you and your children comfortably. And who knows, you may have need of me quite soon. You are used to living so quietly that there is no way of telling you things gently. You should know then that the kind of business your husband does, which is of a fairly modest scale, does not justify an absence which has lasted three weeks already. The journey was certainly not essential, and in any case a week there would have been ample for him to complete his business. It's clear as day that your husband left home intending not to return."

Renée had gone very pale, her nostrils white and pinched. She looked close to fainting.

"You're trying to frighten me," she said weakly. "You're not serious."

"It's possible I'm mistaken and it's only a case of a short dalliance somewhere with a tart. Of course that's the best one could hope for. Has he taken much money with him?"

"On the telephone he told me about a cheque for forty thousand francs that he cashed just before leaving."

"A bad sign. Did he often have affairs, to your knowledge?"

"No, not at all. He had a very regular life and I assure you it would have been difficult to get round my vigilance. I even scared him a little. I am sure that my showing the very smallest hint of suspicion would have been enough to make him break off any liaison, if he ever had one. There are ways of disciplining men in the tiniest elements of everyday life so that they feel as if their wife is always at their side, even when they're far from home."

Talking like this of the power she had over her husband, Renée seemed quite revived and her complexion regained its bloom.

"That's exactly why you should be worried now," I said. "I've known some of these men who are kept nearly dependent by their wives. They are irreproachable until the day when some storm blows them out of their well-trodden conjugal path and then, with their chains broken, there is nothing that can make them come home again. They would rather fall into the direst abjection. I remember one fellow … "

I told her the story of a highly honourable man, a gentleman of comfortable means and father to four children whom he adored, but hopelessly under his wife's thumb, and all to his own misfortune, for after twenty years of marriage, suddenly forgetting his duties for ever, he had run off with a creature who was neither young nor pretty.

"I met him one day in Marseilles, trying to sell boat trips to the tourists in the Vieux Port. He described how he happened to abandon his family. I've never heard a sorrier tale. One evening, on leaving the office, for the first time in his life he yielded to a street girl's charms, and then the idea of meeting his wife's eyes with such a stain on his conscience seemed so terrible that he took a room at the hotel where he had been with the girl. I remember I exhorted him to pull himself together, enlarging on the misery in which he must have left his family: his children scarcely fed, his wife killing herself doing another man's washing, and all the dangers hanging over these creatures whom he still held so dear. But three years after his disappearance he was still under the same spell as on the first day, when his fear alone made him stay in that sordid hotel bedroom."

"Appalling," Renée murmured.

Pensive, she gazed dully at the design of classical drapery that framed the room, and seemed weighed down with a remorse which was not unsatisfying to me. Taking her hands in mine and looking earnestly into her eyes like a true friend, I said:

"Renée darling, already I'm sorry for causing you such anxiety. I ought to have waited a few more days. After all, there was no reason to hurry. Yes, I ought to have waited for you to think of it yourself. I've been stupid. Try to forget a little of what I've just told you, at least for this evening. It is late. Your cousin might return at any moment. I'm going to think some more about this whole business, find out if there are real grounds for our fears, and tomorrow evening, at your apartment, we'll talk again when our heads are clearer."

Renée kissed my neck and told me I could not know how much she loved me. There was something in her tone of voice, something firm and deliberate, which made me think I was becoming a likely choice for a spouse.

XII

I WOKE EARLY THE NEXT DAY, roused by the fear of being caught at home, and I was on the streets by half-past seven. The sky was very clear with no hint of rain, and the air felt unseasonably cold. I began to walk, with no other aim than to ward off the boredom of the long, lonely day that stretched ahead of me. I thought it would be dangerous to return to the office, where Julien might ambush me, and I had given up the idea of continuing to handle business which, as Raoul, I'd had to leave unfinished. Until the evening when I was due to meet Renée, I was sure not to meet a single acquaintance. After an hour of tramping the streets of Paris, I felt a weariness begin to grow in me, which swiftly turned to dejection. I started to consider my adventure with that absence of self-interest which is something like disgust for life when it has become mere habit. I was still indifferent to the absurdity of my situation. I felt for it neither pride nor exaltation of any kind. That morning, it seemed so obvious to me that nothing is more clear-cut, more desperately tedious than that which is unnatural, absurd, incredible, miraculous. Nothing offers less nourishment to the spirit and the senses. I reflected morosely that a miracle is nothing but a dried-out trunk, a stem without roots or boughs. Amazing that the world's religions have found in it independently so certain a manifestation of the divine. What need has God then to oppose, deny, even to hang himself? Seen from this angle, a wonder might be no more than the manifestation of a devil with limited powers, of furtive and restricted means. I even began to think that faith alone could communicate with the imagination and procure the soul's intoxication. I felt that God had abandoned me. I no longer expected anything good to come from my metamorphosis, or even anything that was worth the experience of living through. If things turned out for the very best and Renée consented to follow me, I would have to construct an entirely new life on the basis of a pathetic and embarrassing lie. And in order to back up this fundamental lie, I was condemned to fabricate—and swear by—innumerable others. Indeed, I would need to offer some pretext for leaving Paris, another pretext for refusing to see Uncle Antonin ever again, another to explain why I had no family, why I had to take certain strange precautions, and constantly be ready to answer the most unexpected questions. My children would always consider me an intruder, and might even hate me. Nor could I forget the material difficulties I faced, and I did not feel the necessary resources of energy and invention within me to triumph over them. Renée was capable of enduring such trials with courage but not without bitterness. Her insinuations and allusions to the era of her prosperity would be sure to make our lives unbearable. All that remained for me then would be to abandon wife and children and to begin again from scratch, but already I lacked the will for that. It is hard to be born at the age of thirty-eight, without any excuse or explanation. I had only one real wish: to return to the normal order of things, to win back my right

163

to bend myself to the common rule. I reflected on all this, standing on the railway bridge at Rue Riquet and looking down at the vast landscape of tracks, warehouses and gasometers at my feet, which stretched all the way to the suburbs of Aubervilliers. These outposts of la Chapelle come up to the line of houses that marks out la Villette; their terraced façades are all identical, stained by the trains' smoke, and seemed that day to be nursing incurable cases of psoriasis in the warm sun. A locomotive steamed under the bridge just then and enfolded me in a thick, whitish, stinking cloud that forced its way into my nose and pockets. An insuperable discouragement seized me. It was a pleasure suddenly to give way to it, to offer no resistance. With or without my family, life appeared to me now in the image of this district of railways, warehouses and scabbed houses—a diagram, a pretence, a painted set stuck between changes, a nightmarish armour, a hypothesis, frozen, a region in limbo. I hailed a taxi and gave the driver Julien's address on Rue Copernic. It was half-past nine. Julien was sure to be at home; he always went to bed very late. My visit would surprise him, but there was no doubt he'd welcome the confessions I intended to make him, and without the least astonishment. Since our first encounter he had suspected me of assassinating his friend Cérusier and he now had every reason to believe that his fears were justified. In the taxi on the way to Rue Copernic, I gave myself up to a delicious sense of relief. At last I would be the man the world was entitled to think me; at last I would meet the world's expectations. After my confession, I would have won an existence beyond

164

all doubt, even, most importantly, in my own eyes. My character would be encroached on by no one. Who but myself indeed could account for Raoul's disappearance? I had hardly to play with the words before I had convinced myself that I truly was his assassin.

I was very calm when I rang Julien's doorbell. A lady with white hair and glasses, whom I'd already seen at his house and knew to be his secretary, opened the door to me. "M Gauthier is not at home," she said. My disappointment was so sharp that I was suddenly quite furious.

"That's ridiculous! He never goes out before eleven in the morning!"

"Had you a meeting arranged with him?"

"No. Is there some way of reaching him?"

"He didn't tell me where he was going. I don't think he'll be back home this morning, but perhaps after lunch."

"It's too bad. Would you be kind enough to say that Raoul's assassin came by?"

"I shall not forget," said the secretary gallantly. "M Gauthier will be sorry to have missed you."

I found out later that she took me for an actor who thought it more practical to remind Julien who he was by his part in a film. Moreover, calling myself an assassin like this was not some childish pleasure at causing fright or shock. It was a way of ensuring my own commitment, of refusing the chance I'd been offered to change my mind. The precaution was not unnecessary, since, as I left, I could not help regretting my words. Desperate resolutions ought to result in happiness, without the need to make two attempts at them. Still, mine, in spite of a brief hesitation, was scarcely shaken when I left Rue Copernic, and I headed straight for the Rue du Quatre Septembre. My intention was not to confide in Lucienne. I would not have been brave enough to tell her of Cérusier's death. But I'd had an idea that Julien might be found somewhere near her. There would have to be an occasion of exceptional importance for him to rise at such an early hour. It was quite plausible then, on the day following their first discussion, that they would meet again to look over the information they'd gathered in the intervening time, and would then decide what to do about me.

Recovered from her earlier indisposition, Mme Lagorge informed me that Lucienne was busy in the office with a visitor whose name she had no hesitation in disclosing. It was Julien Gauthier.

"If you wish, I can tell Mlle Lucienne that you are here."

"Thank you. I'm in no hurry. I will wait until she's free."

"It might be a while. M Gauthier is expecting a telephone call."

I sat down in the entrance hall, on one of the two chairs between my office door and Mme Lagorge's window. I could hear the muffled voices of Lucienne and Julien, but did not think to listen to them properly. I didn't really care what was being said next door. I thought calmly about my little piece of drama and felt a pleasant sense of safety, which reminded me of a state of rather silly light-heartedness in which I'd woken one morning intending to wear a brand-new suit that fitted me unusually well. Mme Lagorge answered a telephone call. I heard: "Good morning, yes, please hold the line," and a click.

"It's for M Gauthier," she said, "it's M Fénelon, the handwriting expert."

At those last words, it was as if my blood once more broke into its headlong rush through my veins. Instantly I recovered my fugitive's keenness and agitation. Like an animal caught in a trap and resigned to its end that leaps at a newly opened breach, I woke suddenly from my wise lethargy, all my faculties aroused and tuned to this escape route. Very distinctly, I heard Julien raise his voice and enunciate each of his words separately in order to make himself clear to M Fénelon.

"Hello, yes monsieur. That's very good work. Good. So you confirm that the writing in the letter from Bucharest is identical to that of the sample. Yes, the risk of error is minute. Ah, of course not! That's right. Almost certainly."

Without waiting for the rest, I made for the door, explaining to Mme Lagorge that an urgent errand called me away and that I'd return to the office later on. I swung down the stairs singing, and took the last few steps hopping on one leg. So it had been proven that Cérusier was alive and, short of imagining that he'd got himself locked up somewhere, everything tended to indicate that he really was in Bucharest. At once, I became for the moment an inoffensive character, whom it was pointless to disturb. When Cérusier returned from Bucharest and was told of my activities, he would decide for himself what to do about me. This interpretation, which the expert's findings would naturally suggest to Lucienne and Julien, granted me an important respite. Nothing would be easier than to dispel Uncle Antonin's suspicions. The expert evidence which had just established that Raoul was alive would also prove to Uncle that he no longer existed and that his metamorphosis was a reality. Uncle's attitude the day before, and the isolation that this change consigned me to, had weighed heavily in my fit of despair and I felt that the certainty of recovering his confidence restored my hope. At any rate, his devotion would smooth over a good few obstacles and would help me resolve my problems with Renée without a hitch. Besides, being no longer so pressed for time, I'd have no need to precipitate things.

I walked light-hearted along the Boulevard des Capucines, looking at the passers-by and into the shops with interest. In one window, I caught sight of an advertising sign that announced in large letters: "Visit Romania!" I chuckled mischievously and walked on. A few steps further, I stopped dead, as if at the edge of an abyss. My smile vanished. "Would you be kind enough to say that Raoul's assassin came by?" Those words, delivered only a moment ago to Julien's secretary, resounded suddenly in my head. At first, I knew I was lost. Impossible to take back that unlucky sentence whose impending effect on Julien it was only too easy to predict. Not the slightest doubt that, having heard them and the description the secretary would give of her visitor, he would go straight to the police. I was horribly dispirited, but I would not give way to that depths of discouragement that had led me to accuse myself once already of a crime I had not committed. I remained firmly resolved to assert my innocence, and I sought to reassure myself. After all, it was not completely certain that Julien would see my parting words as an admission of guilt. He might equally see them as an ironic or bitter allusion to his own suspicions—which he'd made clear at the end of our last encounter. Perhaps there was even something I could try, some neat manoeuvre that would incline him towards that particular interpretation. I set to pondering this, but I was in that feverish state when ideas crowd and stream by without any kind of connection, so that it's impossible to pin down a single one. I was walking straight ahead, very quickly, unable to divert my thoughts from the rhythm of my steps. At half-past twelve, I'd thought of nothing worth following up and I refused to let myself stop for lunch until I'd come up with a fruitful idea. This formal injunction led to no better results. I could not imagine any cleverer move than that of going to find Julien and telling him the entire truth.

My meditations had carried me beyond the gates of Paris and, by a quarter past one, I was wandering the streets of a suburb that must have been Asnières, or perhaps Levallois. Exhaustion more than hunger led me to step inside an establishment that looked the epitome of bourgeois provincialism. It contained a billiard table and, on the first floor, a large room for '*Weddings and Banquets*'. The ground floor was itself a large café, the section at the back, on the far side of an isthmus formed by the projection of the counter, serving as a restaurant area at mealtimes. Two tables out of six were occupied when I took my seat at the third. My nearest neighbours were a woman of about thirty years old, dark-haired, buxom, heavily bejewelled, and a man of between fifty and sixty, bald and plump, who was dining beside her. While continuing to eat voraciously, she was firing reproaches at him, her voice thick with phlegm and morsels of food, her dark, rather beautiful eyes sparkling with hatred, and, when momentarily obliged to search for her words, she took great gulps of wine. He looked distressed. He was not hungry and kept saying, "Look here, my kitten, my sweet darling … " Behind his back he was holding a bowler hat which must have fallen to the floor earlier on, and he was flicking at it to dislodge the sawdust that still adhered to its rim. This little trick was irritating his companion. She was saying "Victorien, you've hurt me. It's shameful how you've treated me. The people on the bus were shocked at the way he was looking at my breasts. Everyone was waiting for you to stand up and give him one, but you, you've no more sense of honour than I imagined; all the men in the world could ogle me and you wouldn't lift a finger. Oh, you can see straight away what kind you are! Still, it's shameful for me. Granted it's not the first time someone's looked at me like that. You're not the first man I've had, it has to be said, Victorien. But the main thing is the way they look. And the first thing is that a well-brought-up man does not desire a woman before lunch. You ought to know that, but think about it.

Although you've got money, one can tell you haven't been out much. Leave that hat alone would you, for once?"

I was not in the mood to enjoy a domestic scene. But the rebukes delivered in that phlegmy voice, punctuated by rhythmic swallowing, lulled my anxieties and my fatigue. I envied their absorption in this futile yet vigorous quarrel, safe from the absurdity of a metamorphosis. I would like to have been in that fellow's place. I pictured myself shouting, hurling insults, breaking one of the irascible brunette's teeth with my slap, and—purely for the sake of it—enlivening a row of absolute, reassuring triviality, perfectly rooted in ordinary life. Opposite me, alone in his row of seats, a young man was reading as he ate and, every so often, checking the time on his wristwatch. At a quarter to two, he abandoned his cheese and went to the telephone booth, a tiny room squashed under the staircase that led up to the room for weddings and banquets. The booth lit up and the youth's shadow appeared on the frosted glass of the door. The proprietress was knitting at the bar and smiling graciously at intervals in the direction of the restaurant section. I could hear the muffled ricochet and strike of billiard balls and occasional exclamations from one or other of the players. The young man emerged from the booth, complaining to the waiter that he hadn't managed to get through. Over the next half-hour, he went back several times to redial his number. He looked really troubled and his anxiety reawakened mine. I wondered then if it would be sensible to telephone Julien, but hadn't the strength to make myself do it, drowsy as I was from fatigue and the

171

warmth of the meal. The brunette woman was on to her third dessert and had just ordered more wine. "I'd like to know what you've done to deserve me, that I should give myself to you," she repeated several times and, with another gulp of wine, she didn't hesitate to remind her companion, in particularly insulting terms, of certain ill-favoured aspects of his body which he usually kept secret. Victorien had had enough. "That is absolutely the limit," he declared. He pulled out his wallet and snatched up his bowler. It was all over. For a second she looked terrified, then very tender and, launching herself at Victorien, wrapped her arms around his waist. He struggled: "That's enough, that's enough." She stretched her lips up to the hairy cavity of his purplish ear and spoke to him very softly. He turned his back to me. I saw the skin flush crimson across his bald head and his neck begin gently to sweat inside his detachable collar. It was touching. They ordered coffee and liqueurs; I, coffee and a brandy, which completed my torpor. A billiards player potted four balls consecutively, my neighbouring diners exchanged clumsy blandishments in an undertone, the proprietress succumbed to a fit of coughing, and finally there ensued a space of pure silence. Suddenly the door of the telephone booth opened with such violence that it seemed to explode and the young man leapt out exclaiming:

"The two letters don't have the same handwriting! Raoul from Cambrai has escaped in disguise!"

A loud muttering erupted on the other side of the bar and spread across the room. I realised that everyone was looking at me. Beside me, the couple rose to their feet, their expressions sardonic and menacing. The proprietress, waiter and billiards players advanced along the length of the bar, scolding me in unison. There was nowhere to escape. Sweating with fear, I stood up and ran to safety in the telephone booth. It sounded as if an army was on my heels from the tumult that filled the room. I would have locked myself into the cabin but the door no longer had any hinges and, sliding and wobbling without even a push from me, it constantly had a gaping breach on one side or the other. I pulled a knife from my pocket, but saw that the blade slid backwards into the haft at the slightest encounter with any resistance. Luckily my enemies, who had formed a circle outside my bolt hole, hadn't yet noticed the malfunction of the weapon that held them at bay. With my free hand, I lifted the telephone receiver, but so awkwardly that the wire snapped. From outside the booth, the proprietress said reassuringly: "It doesn't matter, you've only to make your call with the wire, it works just as well." So I dropped the receiver and put my mouth to the dangling wire's end.

"Put me through to God, I beg you," I said.

"Hold the line," replied the voice of Mme Lagorge. "Hello, is that you, my Lord? You have a caller."

"Raoul Cérusier here, from Rue Caulaincourt. My wife has never believed in anything, but as for me, on the contrary, I've always believed."

I waited a couple of seconds, but God didn't answer. I wondered if it would be wise to tell him a lie I'd just thought up, so as to draw his attention, and I resolved to do it almost straight away. I am always much less honest and much less courageous in my dreams than in real life. When I wake up, I'm sometimes annoyed and wonder, "Deep down, perhaps … "

"My dear God," I began again, mournfully, "I scarcely scrape a living and I have five children to feed. It's hard but I still use all my spare time to spread your word. I tell them: the proof that God exists is that bodies attract each other in inverse proportion to the square of the distance between them. See how convenient that square is and how well it works? The power could have been a decimal number. Chance is not prejudiced against whole numbers. So attraction must obey a predetermined law."

"You're not so ignorant," said God, and I realised from his tone of voice that he was flattered, and at the same time I saw him take on the features of one of my old schoolteachers whom I used to taunt a little back then, which reassured me. As he was beginning to demonstrate a geometry theorem, I interrupted:

"How is it that I no longer conjugate with the verb to be?" I asked. "Did you know about this?"

"What? But that's a terrible mistake! exclaimed God. "You are conceived precisely for-for-for—"

Here, anger or distress made him stammer, then lose his legs, his arms, and soon he was nothing but a plaster bust on a mantelpiece and I lost sight of him. The door must have swung back onto its hinges, for it was tightly closed. And now it opened onto an indistinct piece of land with grass growing between the stones and edges that faded into a twilight which may have been a swamp, and which I never remember, even today, without a chill of horror. There was nobody left outside the door except for the proprietress, and now a plain-clothes policeman. Their faces were touched with the artificial light of a warehouse and their clothes were tinted a greyish shade that melted into the décor in places. Neither of them seemed to be bothered about me, but the policeman, turning towards me, announced in a neutral voice: "We've only to pump up the door. I have the recipe here." Straight away, he fitted the mouth of a bicycle pump to the keyhole of my door—as he'd have done to the valve of an inner tube—and set to pumping. At the first puff, the door began to swell and press in towards me like a fattening stomach. I was paralysed with horror. The door's monstrous ballooning pushed me to the back of the cabin and held me there. I wanted to call God, but I had forgotten his name. I was already in my tomb. Soon, I could feel the pressure right across my body but most of all over my stomach, where it seemed the door had become embedded and almost joined up with the partition that I was wedged against. I saw the beginning of my death right there and I sighed: "It's over; forget tomorrow."

The other diners had disappeared. As I slept my head had dropped forward and the table's edge was pressing painfully on my stomach. Standing by the bar, the waiter, looking very correct and bored, was waiting for me to wake. I didn't dare to order another coffee and so I paid and stood up, awkward and somewhat shivery. The sky was overcast and I was surprised by the cold outside.

My disturbed sleep and uneasy digestion left me dazed and indifferent to my morning's preoccupations. I lost my way several times and wasted three-quarters-of-an-hour wandering through soulless streets, at every turn expecting to step back into my nightmare. At last I found myself back at the Porte Champerret, not the Porte d'Asnières which I had been heading for. The walk had not warmed me, but I was very weary. It was just short of four o'clock. I had no difficulty persuading myself that the time to do something about Julien had passed and that he would already have gone out again. It would have been a simple thing to check this, but I was reluctant to enter another telephone booth or even a café, though I would have liked a hot drink. At no other time in my life have I felt so dependent on my digestion. As I passed, a cinema poster attracted me, and, more than that, the need for rest, warmth, oblivion. I hesitated for a moment to lose two more hours to a show in this afternoon of emergencies, then I repeated to myself the words of my dream: "Forget tomorrow."

The film had already begun and I found a seat in the darkness. On the screen, self-confident American youth evolved, discovering love while doing business deals. There was a little clerk, not wealthy but with good prospects, and a pretty typist who was honest and brave and compelled one to feel sympathy and optimism. I forgot my dream in the restaurant. The film theatre's warmth and the pleasure of watching the show soon drove away my discomfort and exhaustion. I felt a sort of confused, rather animal happiness, tainted now and then by the acute awareness that this respite was only temporary. At my side sat a woman with a pleasant scent who seemed to me to be young and elegantly dressed, as far as I could judge in the darkness. When I stooped to retrieve her handbag for her, she thanked me warmly and I remembered that I was handsome. Nothing is further from my tastes and habits than those sordid affairs carried on in the obscurity of film theatres, but a good-looking boy is like one of those people with a beautiful voice: he is tempted to make use of his gift. While I pressed uncertainly against my neighbour, who did not shrink from me but did not encourage me either, reserving her judgement until the interval no doubt, to guard against engaging with a man of unattractive physiognomy or age. While going on like this, I congratulated myself on the prospect of seeing that reserve melt away when the lights went up and revealed the charm and beauty of my face. For the rest, I had no intention of taking things much further, hoping only to leave her a little wistful when we parted at the end of the film. At the interval, my knee and shoulder were still touching hers. I glanced at her first, and saw that I had been lucky with my choice of seat. She was young and pretty, with fine features and elegant clothes. Then she turned to me and I made to meet her eye. Instantly she looked away and, disengaging her knee from mine, drew back to the far side of her seat. She could not have expressed her wish for the game to end more clearly. I was annoyed and somewhat mortified. My experience as a good-looking youth had hardly prepared me for this failure. I tried to console myself with a retrospective contempt, deciding she must be one of those numerous women who, instead of handsome men with attractive, distinguished looks, seem to prefer the heavy, vulgar type of male, whose hirsute meatiness reminds one of an animal.

I left the cinema and caught a bus from Porte Champerret to the Place de Clichy, and then I walked up Rue Caulaincourt. It was half-past seven. I regretted having spoilt my day and, by my cowardice, having aggravated a situation that was already dangerous. Hypocritically, I decided to go home before dinner and to telephone Julien, whom I knew would almost certainly not be at home. As I passed a newsagent I decided to buy an evening paper, and as I was choosing it, the shop assistant told me affably:

"Your wife just bought that one, only five minutes ago."

I excused myself briefly, and so as not to have to explain that she was mistaken, I bought a different paper. As I left, I glanced at the headlines without much interest. I was thinking about the Sarrazine, who would be waiting for me shortly at Café Junot and who would wait in vain, since I was obliged to see my wife that evening. I began to regret my decision. Then, as I came up to my building, I met a local shopkeeper whom I've known for years. He seemed to be in a hurry and called out as he passed, with respectful cordiality: "Good evening, Monsieur Cérusier!"

XIII

NOT WAITING FOR THE LIFT, I raced up the staircase to my fifth floor. There at the door my hand was shaking so violently that I had to make several attempts to fit the key into the lock. It was no longer truly a surprise, but I couldn't help crying out when I saw my old face in the mirror, and I couldn't say today whether it was a thankful cry or one of disappointment. It was, of course, an enormous relief suddenly to be free of a danger which had been hanging over me constantly for the last two days. From now on, I should not be forced to lie, to pretend, to plot endlessly. My cares would be those of an honest man. Sitting on the edge of an armchair, my hands clasped between my knees, I thought without enthusiasm of the habits to which I must return.

From time to time, I rose and looked again into the mirror, perhaps with a small secret hope. My face shocked me, offended my gaze. Until this evening, I had not understood how sullen and heavy, how unappealing I looked. For a second I thought with pain of the face I had just lost. I reproached myself for not knowing how to be worthy of it. My metamorphosis seemed to me like a glorious adventure, a stroke of heavenly favour which I'd been unable to turn to good use. God had taken pity on my deadened state, on the colourless existence to which I had dedicated my life. He had given me a chance to recover my senses, a miraculous chance such as men

179

hardly dare dream of, and yet not once had I recognised the summons to adventure. I had fought for nothing but regaining my wife, my work, my mistress, reassembling the elements of my former life, when I ought to have taken the chance to rid myself of them all. In my new life, I had thought of nothing but retracing old patterns. That very evening, for the sake of my wife, I was preparing to sacrifice a rendezvous with the Sarrazine, a radiant creature whose gaze had never deigned to catch mine before my metamorphosis. I had stood her up deliberately, and not even out of love for Renée, but in the impatient desire to spend an evening at home, to be surrounded once more by my own furniture, my feet in my spousal slippers. Rightly disgusted, God had snatched back my good-looking head.

Obsessed with thoughts of the Sarrazine, images of whom came back to me with superb clarity, I managed to shake myself free by beginning to gather my possessions together. I packed my travelling case, taking care not to include anything Renée might recognise as belonging to her lover. The precaution was not absolutely necessary. However surprised she would have been to see me wearing the guilty watch or the very nightclothes of our sin, she would have been satisfied with my explanations, but I preferred to return free of such mysteries. I divested myself of my new suit, changed my underwear, tie and shoes, and put on the dark grey, striped suit in which I had set off for Bucharest. I was nearly dressed and standing in front of the mirror when Renée telephoned to say she was ready to see me. The maid had gone out and the children were asleep. In a low voice, for I feared I would betray my new transformation, I replied that I would be with her in fifteen minutes. In fact I had nothing left to do in the apartment. I took up my coat, hat and travelling case and stepped out, leaving the key in the lock, on the inside. In a few weeks, the owner, accompanied by a police inspector and a locksmith, would force open the door and look for a corpse underneath the furniture.

Once on the fourth floor, I had only to give the door a gentle push. I was hardly in the hallway when Renée appeared at its far end wearing a white satin negligée trimmed with swan's down—which must have cost the earth. It was time for me to come home. She stood statuesquely in the bedroom doorway, in a pose and light that had evidently been carefully planned. The corridor was still in darkness and I watched her with the joyful anticipation of an ogre. When finally she came to meet me, I pressed the light switch on. She gasped, "Raoul!" and held out her arms. Her face betrayed her confusion. She looked suddenly drawn and pale, her eyes wide and unfocused, but there was nothing in all this that was not explicable by a reasonable emotion and, besides, the disorder lasted no more than a few seconds.

"Darling, I'm so happy," she said in a happy voice, and kissed me. "I was sure you would come back tonight. I felt it ever since I woke up." She stepped back a pace and, showing me her new negligee, added in a low, coy voice with just a hint of mischief, "You see: I was waiting for you."

Renée, as shown on numerous occasions, was by her

nature disgusted by unnecessary lies. It hurt me to see the ease with which she pronounced this one.

"It's charming," I said, visibly reluctant despite my efforts.

As we entered the bedroom, Renée asked me if we had closed the front door properly. "Yes, I think so," I replied, with a hesitation that was calculated to leave her doubtful.

"I'm going to make sure."

"In a moment. There's no rush. Who do you think might come in at this hour? Tell me how the children are."

Renée did not dare to insist. She smiled and spoke calmly, but her voice trembled once or twice, and I caught her glancing furtively towards the corridor. This went on for nearly a quarter-of-an-hour, until, having taken my coat, she went to hang it up in another room. Then I heard the front door slam. She need no longer fear her lover's approach on tiptoe in the darkness and his tender scratch on the bedroom door. I thought now that her face emanated tranquillity. She was sitting in an armchair, one leg across the other, and as she spoke, her white leather slipper swung from the toes of her dangling foot. This casual attitude and the warm, attentive gaze she fixed on me made me regret ending her punishment so soon. As she was asking about my stay in Bucharest, I indicated that she should be quiet and whispered urgently: "Someone just knocked." Renée rose with such suddenness that her slipper flew off. Without stopping to put it back on, she tried to limp ahead of me to the bedroom door. "I'll go," she said, "you stay where you are."

"But look darling, you're not dressed."

I was already in the corridor. She took one step into it herself and, in a ringing tone which ought to have been audible from the floor above, pronouncing my name with great clarity, she called to me:

"I beg you, Raoul, don't go out there. It might be dangerous, Raoul."

After glancing around the landing, I shut the door and returned to my wife, who was already back in her armchair, her slipper replaced. She looked up at me with an affectionate smile. The conversation recommenced where we had left off. I sensed that Renée was enjoying the lighthearted spirit and lucid quickness that spring from knowing one has manoeuvred successfully out of a danger.

"So all in all," she said, "your journey was completely pointless."

"Obviously, the results have not been brilliant and I had hoped for better. Everything went against me. I couldn't have foreseen that the markets were going to collapse three days after I left. I've had to play a very unlucky hand."

"Never mind. Besides, you can't be blamed for being one of those who didn't predict it. There have to be some who don't. What I don't understand is why after the third day, when you knew the likely chances for business, you didn't come home straight away."

"I couldn't, I assure you. There was always the hope of initiating something that would justify my journey."

"My poor dear, you'll never change. But it doesn't matter; I'm so happy you're back."

She was smiling at me kindly, indulgently. I realised that I had just defended myself like a guilty man. Renée's observations were so much part of her manner and I was so accustomed to receiving them with my usual timidity that at the very next occasion I had once again bowed to her influence and, forgetting my superiority as her husband, I had willingly submitted. I resented it belatedly, for the conversation was already over.

"What a lovely welcome," I said, chuckling grimly. "I return after three weeks' absence only to have my wife reproach me for my naivety and conclude that, alas! I'm always the same. What a pleasant thing to hear. I'm made to feel that I come in like a spoilsport who can't be dealt with any other way."

That last line sounded to me adroit and disturbing in just the right degree. Delivering my little speech, I pictured—along with my stance—my frowning expression, which I felt to be a perfect companion and catalyst of my meaning. I had forgotten the most important thing. My half-conscious image of myself was still that of the man I had ceased to be a few hours ago. I realised my mistake on meeting the eyes of my actual face in a mirror. This reassertion of reality was a painful and humiliating surprise, and I was infuriated.

"Raoul, look, that's ridiculous. You know very well you're being unfair," said Renée, on a note of affectionate reproach.

"Yes, ridiculous, I know, you've no need to tell me. I knew a good while ago precisely how you see me, the kind of man I represent to you. Ridiculous, perfectly ridiculous. And dull, isn't it? Dull and coarse. I know you made a mistake when you married me. I know that all these years we've been together, you've been making do, making the best of it. I lack understanding, charm, everything that makes a woman's life pleasant. I'm a dullard. At least I've no illusions on that score. If you've found the strength to live with such a mediocre husband, you've not had enough to keep me from knowing how you see me. Or rather, you judged me too dull to understand."

Renée had risen and was staring at me uncomprehendingly. Such was her surprise at hearing her own complaints, and in the very same terms she had pronounced them, that she didn't even think to protest. She could only shrug helplessly, and my fury increased.

"You are right. Contempt always was effective with me. Go on. Why trouble yourself? The good old dullard that I am will accept everything. No fear of his hitting back. There's a way of disciplining men in the tiniest details of everyday life which puts them once and for all in thrall to their wives. It's well conceived. But a day will come when, in spite of everything, we see that there are other things to do in life than fawn like a dog at the feet of a good, po-faced little woman. Look, you ought to know. I didn't go to Bucharest for business, but because I'd had enough of your bedchamber and your neat, well-dusted heart. I had gone meaning never to come back. And I had a wonderful journey, a journey you wouldn't understand with that little accountant's head of yours. What kind of regret, what idiotic scruple made me return to

185

this airless hole! Life had become so wide, so plentiful; I had so much to do, to attempt, and yet I had to come back to imprison myself here, to gather dust, to go numb and dead to the world."

I was intoxicated with anger and regret. I saw rivers, vines at harvest, tropical forests, tower blocks and Chinese ornaments. I thought of the Sarrazine, I called to her in despair. Frightened by my revelations at first, Renée now began to recover her dignity and was already racking her mind for one of those clever, cutting ripostes which were her speciality. Inspiration lit her cool eyes, which were screwed up with the effort of thinking of it, but as she opened her mouth, I turned away and called over my shoulder on my way out:

"That's it, I'm leaving."

Renée screamed, ran after me and cried out again, sobbing. It was no good, nothing could have made me stay. I was going back to Bucharest; I was starting my life again. Outside, without hesitation and almost without thinking about it, I strode up Avenue Junot. It had just rained and the road and street lights were still wet. A shivering down-and-out with a burnt-out cigarette butt between his lips asked me for a light. As I walked past without stopping, he remarked mournfully: "It's always that way. Even when it doesn't cost them a penny."

I saw the Sarrazine the moment I walked into the Junot. She was alone at the far end of the room, reading a newspaper and stirring her coffee. At the sound of my steps she looked up, then straight away went back to her reading. I sat down at a table facing hers. I watched her, constrained by a sorry sentiment of regret and also by a kind of senseless hope. Her angled face, which I saw as if from above, seemed illuminated by a deep-felt joy. Often, without raising her head from her paper, she looked towards the door, and her black eyes reflected the anxiety of her vigil. I said to myself: "It's me she's waiting for. It's me she's thinking about." Looking at her, I suddenly saw my own face in the mirror above her shoulder. I forced myself only to see hers and went on waiting for a miracle. The Sarrazine folded her newspaper and looked up. As she looked round the room, her glance fell for a second on me, unseeing, as if on a dead object. I felt as if I were being buried alive, struggling under a crushing weight, unable to draw attention to my presence. I managed to leave my seat and walk over to her. She frowned, thinking me some kind of meddler.

"Madame," I murmured. "Excuse me. Sarrazine?" Surprised and unnerved more than anything, she nodded. I had approached her without knowing what I would say and the situation obliged me to utter words that went counter to all my hopes. In spite of myself, I went on: "My friend Roland Colbert has asked me to convey his apologies. He has had to leave France suddenly and doesn't expect to return for some time. He confessed to me that he was very unhappy not to tell you himself. He had, I believe, neither your name nor your address."

The Sarrazine seemed crushed by the news and looked down to hide her distress. I felt as if for her it was more than mere disappointment—a real affliction. Annoyed to have let me see this, she rallied and looked back at me with some curiosity, to see the face of her lover's chosen confidant. Her expression remained cold; I imagine I disappointed her. I was briefly tempted to tell her that I had lost my real face and that I was the miserable victim of an incredible metamorphosis, but a confession like that could only make me ridiculous. I contented myself with the humble suggestion:

"If you like, when I have some news from him, I could let you know."

The Sarrazine did not answer. A poignant silence settled between us. Then, glancing at her watch, she leant back slightly and, with a courteous smile, thanked me for my trouble. It was over.

I returned to my table and paid for my drink without sitting down again. I could not help looking back when I reached the door. One elbow on the table, her chin cupped in her hand, she was looking straight ahead and slowly exhaling cigarette smoke. I lingered for a few seconds, still hoping she might call me back and ask me to talk about him, but she paid me no more attention.

The rain had begun to fall once more, a wearying torrent of dense drops that exploded as they touched the asphalt. The man who had asked for a light had taken refuge on the Junot's deserted terrace, where I was sheltering too. He didn't seem to recognise the pedestrian who was too busy to stop for him, and said cautiously: "It's the season for it, anyhow." We exchanged a few remarks and, before going on my way, I gave him some cigarettes and a box of matches which he accepted with particular pleasure. Thinking I took him for a tramp—

which he almost certainly was—he had the delicacy to reassure me.

"I'm not from this neighbourhood," he said. "I live much nearer Bercy really. Pretty often, you find yourself far from home, without the faintest idea why. You come and you go, isn't that it? And, in the end, you find yourself far away from home."

It was raining less heavily. I turned up the collar of my coat and ran down Avenue Junot. I went back home without any more sense of purpose than I'd had on going to meet the Sarrazine. The life of adventure I had begun a quarter-of-an-hour before had come to an end of itself. And it wasn't due to the rain either. My adventure's conclusion, which was beyond my control, obliged me to go home and I went meekly, like a man who has nothing else to do. Opening the door, I saw Renée standing as she had before at the far end of the corridor. She had exchanged her white satin negligée for a flannelette nightgown. Rather than go to her, I looked into the children's bedroom. They were both asleep. Toinette was tucked in with her doll, which took up most of the space in her little bed. Usually we would rescue the doll, lifting it from the bed once Toinette was asleep. This evening it had been forgotten. Lucien was invisible except for a mop of tousled hair that was sticking out from between his bedclothes. I stood there for a moment, looking at them and listening to their breathing. It seemed as if life were returning to its natural rhythm, and at last I could feel unmixed joy to have recovered the face with which I might kiss my children in the morning. I smiled indulgently to myself, thinking that only a moment ago I had gone for ever, to live life as I wished.

I found Renée outside in the corridor, standing with her back to the front door. She thought I had returned only to make my last goodbyes to the children. Her face was set, her gaze direct.

"Raoul," she said. "You must listen to me. I won't ask you to stay, don't worry, but I have something to confess to you."

I was troubled, quite lost for words. How should I respond to her confession? I gestured helplessly in protest.

"Just then," she continued, "you left the house having accused me unjustly. You put yourself in the wrong. That a man may be irritated by his wife and by faults which he has always known is no reason to leave her. You take a very wicked part in doing this. But you do have a reason to leave me, a real reason, and I want you to know it for your peace of mind and for my own as well. I've been unfaithful to you. While you were away, I've had a lover."

"I know."

Renée stopped, stunned into silence. The situation amused me and I was smiling—not out of bitterness, as Renée doubtless believed, but through simple good humour. I managed to put on a serious expression, doing my best to convey an Olympian gravity and aloofness.

"Of course I know it. Do you think you could hide something like that from me for a minute? I saw it coming; it was in your eyes, your attitude. I recognised it in every word you spoke. Women have many ideas regarding their ability to lie. In fact, their skill lies mostly in sweetening the pill, and the man who won't put up with being deceived knows exactly where he stands. I was sure even before seeing you again. When I called you the last time from Bucharest—it was last Friday—I realised what had happened from a change in your voice and your manner."

My wife stared at me in astonishment and, I had no doubt, began to see me in a new light.

"One is always wrong to despise one's husband. As soon as you despise someone, you stop understanding them and then you're at their mercy. I saw it just now. You thought you could treat me with a kind of casual superiority and yet every one of your words and gestures was a confession which even now you would hesitate to tell me directly. I have learnt more about your adventure than even you know, my child, and it isn't too much to say that your confession, if we grant it's sincere, won't reveal anything new to me. Besides, you're not telling me the whole truth when you say: 'I've had a lover'—you should be saying: 'I have a lover'."

Renée protested that it was all over, protested vehemently, but her voice lacked conviction.

"If everything really is over between you," I said, "it's only been so in the last quarter-of-an-hour. I would bet that your lover does not even know of your decision to break with him. What is certain is that the man you were expecting this evening was not me. And you had no hesitation making this your rendezvous, without a thought for the children. Perhaps they even know him, this person, and you have made them into accomplices. Oh, in the name of God, if I had known."

I was truly very angry. Renée shook her head and began to weep. Seeing her like this, humiliated and miserable, I thought with pride of the years I had spent trembling in the fear of displeasing her or not agreeing with her. I held out my handkerchief – for she was mortified and close to tears – and drew her back from the door.

"Don't stay there. Someone might go past on the landing and hear us."

Sniffling and sobbing, Renée walked before me, dragging her feet. Proud and terrible as a judge, I on the other hand pretended to have a slight cold and coughed several times in frightening explosions. I told her to sit in the armchair where only a short time ago she had played with her white slipper—which was far off now, in the depths of some drawer along with the satin negligée. She sank into it, enveloped in flannelette and tears, facing me on the edge of the bed. It was my turn to speak. I said, "In God's name," one more time, to serve as a reminder and bridge, and then:

"It's unbelievable. That it should come to this, you, the mother of my children. And perhaps that's not the worst of it. When I remember the scene you were acting when I arrived. Poor, unhappy, pitiful creature! Oh, it's not the lie itself that disgusts me. When, instead of the lover one is expecting at home, with one's children, one sees one's husband appear, one *has* to lie. What has torn me apart, what I'll never forget, is seeing you, normally so honest and so frank, lying light-heartedly, with relish, yes, that's

it: relish. I saw you drunk with the joy of your own deg-
radation, your own corruption. Ah, you poor woman,
unable to comprehend what I have suffered at the sight
of this—this, well, of this sight."

Through her tears, Renée began to splutter and
stammer: "Raoul, forgive me—been unworthy—never
again—Raoul, forgive."

Raoul—I—stood up and paced around the room, taking large, thoughtful strides while scratching my head
or supporting it with one fist under the chin; that head
which was to make such a serious decision. The silence
did not bother me. I let it drag on and on. Eventually:

"For the sake of the children," I said, "so be it. I'm
happy to agree to some form of communal life. We should
behave for them as if nothing has happened. At least, I
will do my best. Of course, there's no question of our
ever sleeping together again."

I hesitate to tell what followed; it came to me in a
sudden inspiration. If I succeed, I will have achieved a
superb act, a miracle beside which my metamorphosis
will be nothing. I bite the bullet—I say:

"On the days when I happen to sleep at home, such as
this evening, I shall sleep in the blue bedroom."

I've spoken loudly, with my back to my wife. I dare to
turn round. She is looking at me in respectful admiration
and complete devotion. I am master. I stroll once more
round the room with my big strides. I stop, to tell my
wife: "I'm tired."

"I'll go and make up your bed," she says in a docile
little voice with just a hint of entreaty. She stands up at

once and disappears into the corridor after a timid last glance at me. I am, all the same, an impressive figure. I go to look at myself in the mirror, to reconcile myself finally to my good old Cérusier face.

XIV

I WHISTLED WHILE I DRESSED. My wife came to make sure I had everything I needed. For the first time in my life, I gave the maid who carried in my tray a great friendly clap on the back, and it was great fun. "All under control, Marguerite?" "Yes, sir," and she smiled from ear to ear.

Here come the children. They kiss me, pull me along with them, squash my head between their two little heads, do their best to tear me limb from limb. I give a great loud Cérusier guffaw. That's me. I tell them about Bucharest, and about the aeroplane. When it's time for school, I leave with them. Toinette goes to the local nursery school which is just the other side of the junction, fifty metres away. During these last three weeks, I could have watched her coming and going from my fifth-floor windows, but I hadn't thought of it. She kisses me outside the school, hanging on to me for a second, then runs off to her class. Lucien goes to the Lycée Rollin on the other side of Montmartre. We climb Rue Girardon together. He confides that he wants to become a naturalist and talks excitedly about M Colbert, a new tenant in the building, whom they met at the museum and who knows everything about antediluvian animals. Jealous, I seize the chance to cool his enthusiasm.

"Fifteen hundred litres of milk? But that's completely wrong. Megatheriums produced no more than two hundred litres. My boy, I don't think your naturalist can be a very serious one. I even consider it rather a mark of dishonesty to take advantage of a child's credulity in order to spout such nonsense. He's as much a naturalist as I'm an archbishop. When I see him, I shan't hesitate to give him a piece of my mind."

Lucien retains a solid faith in the extent of my wisdom, but he's sorry about the fifteen hundred litres and he sighs. Once again, he remembers that you should always hide all discoveries that are at all exciting from your parents. And never expect them to supply any marvellous secrets. On our way, we meet a boy from Lucien's class, Alain Leduc, whom he invites to join us.

"You know," says Lucien, "what I was telling you the other day about the megatherium making fifteen hundred litres of milk—it's not true. Papa just told me. It wasn't fifteen hundred, it was two hundred."

"Oh," says Leduc politely, and I see from his expression that my opinion carries no weight with him at all. Instead I sense a determined hostility and even a secret scorn directed at me. Doubtless he has spread the news of the fifteen hundred litres among his comrades, or he intended to, and he doesn't mean to renounce the pleasure of amazing them and of being amazed himself so easily. My prestige as father, which convinced Lucien, hasn't the slightest effect on Leduc.

After leaving the boys, I make my way into town on foot. My body feels refreshed, my heart relieved, and as I walk, I have a sense of lightness and renewal that brings to mind my clearest memories of childhood. I think also of my bleak expedition yesterday through La Chapelle and the autumnal streets of the suburbs beyond. This morning, I've no need to call up God on the telephone. He is in me, as he is in all men, and I am his creature once more. My life and my face are the ones he gave me to do as I please with. I am like everyone else and I'm glad of it. I start to smile at some pretty girls in the street; they don't notice me and I laugh at my own presumption. For a short moment, I feel an apple tree inside me break into flower, an apple tree from when I was six, which consoled me one day when I had to go to school. It's no good trying to summon it up. If it flowers again, as this morning, it is never at my request. On the Rue des Martyres I buy a bunch of violets for Lucienne and, suddenly eager to see her again, I take a taxi.

I am first to arrive at the office; it's not yet half-past eight. The memory of yesterday's scene weighs on my mind somewhat and I fear its consequences today.

Always punctual, Lucienne enters the main hall. I hear her walk into the next-door room and she starts to sing, her boyish voice slipping out of tune now and then. I take two or three steps towards the door that separates us and stop there, anxious. The words I uttered at our last meeting rush back to me with painful clarity: "He told me everything, absolutely everything, I tell you. Oh, I won't repeat everything he said. There are still some things I would not do. But, I assure you, there's nothing Cérusier wouldn't do." I feel the shame mount in my cheeks at the thought that Lucienne would believe all these confessions. I hide the bunch of violets I've just bought in my pocket, and I would like to hide myself as

I did on the first evening of my metamorphosis in the boxroom or in the shadow of the cupboard doors. I'm a little reassured as I remember that in the conversations he must have had with Lucienne, Julien Gauthier would have shared his conviction that Roland Colbert must have seen Cérusier's private diary. No one could begrudge the author those confidences he made only to himself. Unfortunately, it is hardly likely that Lucienne would believe in the existence of this secret diary. Julien, being a man, is easily satisfied with such theoretical possibilities. Not Lucienne. Without a doubt, her first thought would have been to examine the material circumstances of such an enterprise. She knows it would have been impossible for me to keep such a secret diary at home, and at work I couldn't have done it without her knowledge, or at least, without rousing her curiosity by strange habits which today would prompt her to say: "Indeed, now I understand why … " She knows too that I am not the kind to keep a diary and, unlike Julien, she thinks this counts for something. Nevertheless, I hope she will harbour some favourable doubt.

She comes into my room singing and I'm almost reassured, so I greet her with confidence. Once she's recovered from the surprise, she tells me that she's glad I've returned and we shake hands warmly. In the taxi on the way to Rue du Quatre Septembre just now, I was dreamily imagining a sweet embrace, but I sense from the beginning that something has changed in her manner towards me. She smiles, pleased to know what's become of me, but not overjoyed to see me once more. It seems too that she is taking care in subtle ways to keep me at a distance.

Nevertheless, her attitude is open and friendly. I see not the slightest reproach in her bright, honest eyes, nor any distrust: only at times a troubled look, and then her words falter and she blushes. Our effusions, or what we show of them, are swiftly concluded and we quickly move on to business matters. Once on this safe territory, all embarrassment disappears. I imagine that only my shyness and still-burning shame led to that early constraint between us, and I prepare to tell her what I've been thinking since the moment I informed my wife that I would no longer regularly sleep at home. The arrival of Mme Lagorge, who is late by a good half-hour and feels obliged to welcome me back and present her excuses, stops me speaking. Before going into the next room to give the typist her morning's task, Lucienne asks me to telephone Julien Gauthier.

"He wants to see you as soon as possible. It's about something very serious."

I put on a surprised, enquiring look.

"It's really very serious," Lucienne repeats.

"You know what it's about?"

"Yes, M Julien Gauthier has already discussed this business with me, but I would rather not say anything to you myself. I would be afraid of putting it clumsily and of warning you in the wrong way. It's better that your friend tell you himself."

"Right. I must see him straight away. Would you find out if he's at home?"

Turning into Rue Copernic, I still haven't managed to decide what to do. I could simply listen to Julien and then thank him profusely. I could also try to make him admit the truth. The former is of course the easier and wiser course, but I feel I owe it to our friendship not to hide anything from him. Besides, I would like to restore my wife's good name. Yet there remains the difficulty of conveying a truth which is no less absurd today than it seemed three weeks ago. On the threshold of Julien's building, I remember my conversation with Lucien about the milking capacity of the megatherium. I think of the ease with which I made him renounce a belief which had been valuable to him, and of my failure to do the same with his friend Leduc. I would like to believe that Julien Gauthier's trust will serve me as well and that his friend will be able to make himself understood where the stranger could only arouse the most dangerous suspicions. Anyway, I don't think I run any great risks if I try.

Julien, who's in the middle of getting dressed and still wearing his nightshirt, receives me in his bedroom.

"Old man, you've no idea how happy I am to see you again. I almost didn't dare to hope I would. I've never had you so much on my mind as these last weeks. Sit down. I'll just shave then I'll be back."

His joy at my return is sincere, and I am moved. This affectionate welcome confirms my resolution. Over the last few days, his friendship has led him to such devotion and anxious zeal on my behalf that I would be ashamed to repay him with a lie. I sit down on the unmade bed, just as I did in the days when I used to turn up and surprise him in his hotel room. I can hear him singing as he shaves and I notice that his voice has a girlish tone which hardly suits his style. Shaven at last, he takes a chair facing me.

"What can you have been up to in Bucharest for three weeks? I was wondering that just last night, going to bed. I thought: he must have cleared off with a bird—if not, well, my poor friend!

"I didn't go to Bucharest. I never left Paris."

"That's a bit much. You didn't leave Paris? Are we allowed to know why you went into hiding?"

"But Julien, I didn't hide," I said gently.

He sees by my voice and eyes what is meant by these simple words. His whole body speaks his astonishment; he is like one of Rembrandt's pilgrims standing before the Saviour risen from the dead and shining with the light of the miracle. We are silent, gazing at each other. Eventually, I say, shrugging despondently:

"What can I do, what's true is true. On my way to see you here, I wasn't sure whether I should be completely honest. It would have been so simple to say nothing, so restful to leave behind this whole ridiculous story. And then I thought: no. I must not hide the truth from the one man who has spent these three weeks in such brotherly anxiety. Yes, Julien, the man in the café whom you took for a madman and whom you suspected of wanting to assassinate me—that was me. But today, I can't even call on our shared memories to persuade you, nor on my voice or my scar. There is no proof at all that my face has twice been changed. There's only me here to tell you."

201

I fell silent. In fact, I exaggerated my lack of resources. I could have cited certain key presumptions. For example, we could easily have returned to the office for specimens of Roland Colbert's handwriting, which was disguised but which an expert would instantly recognise as mine. Yet my experience of the absurd keeps me from asserting anything which would be the beginnings of a proof, for the best-planned arguments achieve nothing in this field except for stirring up hopes and setting in motion the hazardous mechanism of reason. The advocate of the absurd must, as artists do, address the parts of men that demonstration and eloquence can't reach, and something tells me that in this matter everything depends on the simplicity of your method. Even now I may have said too much. I ought to have kept to just a few words. However, Julien is looking at me keenly, leaning towards me as if he's trying to 'catch' a radio signal.

"I believe you," he says, almost under his breath and a little guiltily.

A sweet and powerful emotion grips me and makes the tears flow down my cheeks. I say: "It's stupid." Julien takes my hands in his and squeezes them affectionately.

"Forgive me, Raoul. I've been an idiot. No more sense than a policeman. And to think that you called on me for assistance and that I, vain fool, refused you, cut you off. You were in trouble and instead of helping you I made your troubles worse. My friend, what remorse. My punishment is having missed an adventure that I could have lived through with you. Tell me."

I begin to tell him everything, from the photographs onwards. Fascinated, Julien follows my tale with complete attention, and sensing his immersion in the story, I warm to my recital. He admires Uncle Antonin for his instant acceptance of my metamorphosis. "What a man, what a youthful outlook," he sighs. I describe those changes of disposition, perhaps more superficial than profound, that I had experienced and which I had ascribed to the influence of my new face. He cannot forgive himself, he who knows me so well, he says, for not having been there to judge how real they were. Talking about Lucienne and how I behaved towards her over the three weeks, I decide not to tell Julien of our intimacy and I attribute everything to a clash of temperaments, as if Roland Colbert were simply jealous of Cérusier's authority over the young woman. In fact, the affection that ties me to Julien is strong enough for me not to hesitate and this discretion allows me to calm a troubled spot on my conscience.

From Julien, I learn little of significance about his movements over the last few days.

"After the handwriting evaluation," he says, "I was told that the individual"— he laughs—"visited my apartment yesterday morning, calling himself Raoul's assassin—which reassured me. I only saw in that the irritated gesture of a fellow who felt himself unjustly suspected. You see, I was hardly ready to think you'd just accused yourself of a crime. What a shame. When I think of how terrible that day was for you and what agonies I made you live through, I'm disgusted with myself. I will never forget what a dunce I have been, from beginning to end of this whole affair. A pretentious dunce. I'm afraid you still blame me for it, a little."

"My dear fellow, blame you? On the contrary, I'm grateful for everything you tried to do to stop me—it's a proof of our friendship. But I have something to ask you and it concerns you personally. I'm curious to know how it affects you to think that something as absurd as this has actually happened. I've been too involved in the story to conceive what an observer might feel, confronted with what I think we're obliged to call a miracle. How do you handle it yourself?"

Julien thinks for a second. He is clearly concerned not to say anything that isn't true.

"Well, here you are. I have to admit that I look with a certain detachment, you could even call it indifference, on something which really ought to shock me profoundly, which ought to overwhelm me. Of course, this is not about what you suffered; that I can well imagine for myself. But the fact of the metamorphosis, which should make my mind boggle, simply leaves me stunned, and ultimately quite calm. I don't believe it is a lack of imagination. I see very well what you might excuse by a loophole like that, but I haven't the strength."

He allows himself another moment's thought and then goes on:

"If you were to ask me why I believe in the metamorphosis this time, I would answer that I have three reasons. The first and most convincing is that you are my good old friend Raoul Cérusier whom I have known for the last twenty years to be an honest fellow and hardly given to imaginative indulgence. The second—and slightly less decisive—reason may help to explain why I'm not as shocked as you expected. Something that helps me believe in your miracle is that it is over, it is in fact already in the past. I may be wrong, but what is staggering for me about a miracle is its presence, its nearness; then I am forced to play some part in its world. I can encounter it, see it mingle with my life. If on the contrary it is no longer happening, it no longer involves me, or scarcely. It's like a railway disaster: you can't be moved now if it's ancient history. In short, the fact that your metamorphosis is already over allows me to work things out according to my reason, which at this point doesn't feel too seriously threatened. Above all, you mustn't think I've come to any kind of rational compromise. But reason is like a guard dog, barking and tugging on its chain when prowlers appear at his perimeter fence, but keeping its muzzle shut or giving just the mildest growl when they stay clear."

"Yes, I understand, but that's not very reassuring. If instead of this story, which is already done and dusted, I'd come to tell you about a completely new metamorphosis—to tell you for example that a woman has been changed into a swallow—your good sense would not have allowed you to believe your old friend."

"I don't know," said Julien. "That's quite a tall order for a metamorphosis. You might as well tell me that when it comes to the absurd, the degree of it makes no difference, it remains a question of presentation, of how you dress it up and of the circumstances. And I would have been perfectly able to believe you anyway. Obviously the swallow idea would have set my reason barking, but if I needed convincing I would have made sure not to hear its howls. I would have got round it with a fit of exaltation, or through some poetic or mystical transport, or even by going mad. But you ask me this now and, fundamentally, I have nothing unusual to teach you. People who believe in the absurd are ten a penny. I know people who believe in ghosts, others who believe in black magic or in seances. At some point in their lives they have found themselves facing the same problem I had just now and most of them handled it by becoming a little cracked or, if you prefer, by overcoming their common sense. Far more interesting, I think, is what you think, having lived this yourself and been the object of the miracle. Your certainty is still of a particular quality, and as disgusting as it seems to you, you have been focusing on it for some time."

"Ah well, there I must disillusion you: I don't think the thought of my metamorphosis has a large place in my life. You know me—I'm a bit dull. I'm not one of those to lose their heads on meeting a slightly unusual truth. I know better than anyone what to do with difficult questions when they bother me. My own common sense has none of those susceptibilities that need to be managed ingeniously. Up to the age of twenty, I was a literalist and committed Catholic. I really believed that Joshua stopped the sun in its path and yet I knew that the earth turns around the sun. I never struggled to find a trick by which to reconcile these things. My reason must work in separate compartments, as it does in so many people, and probably in those who believe in ghosts or black magic and who seem to you a little confused. There must be a compartment for my metamorphosis, and when I happen to remember it or to think about it at all, my life won't be the least bit troubled. Moreover, during these weeks when my head was indeed in turmoil, I was much more preoccupied by the consequences of the metamorphosis than by the miracle itself, as such. Ultimately, I stand by what I thought yesterday evening, having got my real face back: this adventure was not for me."

"In that case," observed Julien, "nor am I the ideal confidant. You might have been lucky enough to confide in someone more explosive, who would have gone into a trance and reeled off a string of ' … but then, then what … ' Although to think of it, I can't picture any well-balanced man get very worked up about your adventure. A miracle by itself, with nothing going for it but its absurdity—why that's hardly exciting."

We talk for two hours and more and soon it's nearly midday. I remind Julien that he's not dressed and that I'd arranged yesterday evening for both of us to join Uncle Antonin for lunch at a restaurant in Porte Maillot. The poor man certainly won't be expecting to see me back with my old face. I've decided to tell him that I really am just back from Bucharest, ignorant and innocent of the whole drama. Julien thinks this unfair, and I concede that Uncle deserves better treatment. But if I tell him the truth this time, I'll have no decent reason to make him keep it secret. Not only will he be unable to refrain from publicly proclaiming such big news, but he will consider it his duty to testify to it. He will broadcast to our family and friends the news that I stole the looks of a bright-eyed young god in order to go to bed with my wife. An attractive prospect. I can just see my cousin Hector's smile as he learns of what he would call a poetic translation. After all, no matter what Uncle could make of his revelation, I will not at any price allow my life to be dominated by an adventure which, on the contrary, I intend to consign to the past. My return from Bucharest will cut short all further developments in that vein. Eventually, Julien agrees with me.

"I can't help thinking about it," he says, as he dresses. "Just now, examining the elements which went into my conversion to the absurd, I said there were three of them, but I see that I've forgotten to mention the third. Would you like to know it? Well, my boy, I reckon the third is to be found in a particularly good mood which is making me more gullible than usual. Yes, I think that joy and happiness in being alive have made me less vigilant, and thus more amenable to the logic of the heart. I am so happy."

Sitting on the bed, I turn round to face him. Julien, in his shirtsleeves, a tie in one hand, is smiling blissfully.

"Are you in love?"

"Yes. In love with the most beautiful, with the purest girl. An orchard in April. Raoul, I'm getting married. I've said enough already for you to guess who she is. I'm in love with Lucienne."

I feel myself go bright red. He's still wearing his idiotic smile. I'd like to slap him.

"Does she love you too?"

"Yes, she loves me. Everything was decided yesterday evening. I should tell you that we've seen each other quite often, these last three weeks. The day after your metamorphosis, I went to ask her for more information about your trip to Bucharest. The following day I ran into her accidentally. I went back to your office several times. Then we went to the cinema a few times, and to the theatre. Then, when I saw you with your wife on Boulevard Saint-Germain, I decided to tell her about the dangerous individual, and together we feared for your life. That evening we dined together. I scarcely left your office after that. And there you are. A moment ago, I was thinking: good old Raoul. It's thanks to his journey to Bucharest that we are so happy. And now I can say: it's thanks to your metamorphosis. That's much more beautiful. Don't you think?"

I reply—yes, indeed. He praises Lucienne at length, speaks to me of her simplicity of heart, her honesty, her sweet gaze and fresh complexion. He is inexhaustible. Dressed at last, he leaves me in the room for a moment alone, crushed by this new blow. I have just lost something very precious to me—Lucienne's love; I have also lost my reason for adopting the new lifestyle I'd planned for myself. I thought about not returning home this evening. I had already set aside my Sundays. From midday on Saturday I had thought we would set out, cycling or even on foot. I had dreamt of making love in the woods. When it rained or on cold winter days: the fireside, a cosy apartment, tea for two and the cinema. I would say to my wife: "I'll be back by Monday evening." And in Rue Caulaincourt, at Manière's, at the Rêve, they'd be saying, "Well I never, didn't you know? Cérusier has a mistress now." They'd be saying, too, "See how he dresses these days, he's quite the dandy, and isn't it wonderful how young he's looking too." They would be right. The joy of being in love would restore my youth. And I loved Lucienne so much—her sweetness, tall body, primrose scent. I was ready to devote my life to her. For example, one day she would fall ill. The doctor would say, we need a blood transfusion, three litres minimum. I would be there, I'd offer my blood. When the three litres were taken and used up, the doctor would say, we need one more litre. Already dying, I would answer, take as much as you need, you've only to take it, so willing that in the end he would take it all. But Lucienne would be saved and I would be lucky and survive too. Then she would adore me as no other woman ever loved a man, and our love would be the envy of all around us.

That evening I would go home—that evening, the next, and every evening after that. On Sunday, Renée and I would take a walk in the Bois de Boulogne, have an aperitif on the Champs-Elysées, and grenadines for the children; next Sunday it would be the Bois de Vincennes, or a trip to the Roman amphitheatre. I see something bulging out of my trouser pocket. It's the bunch of violets bought this morning for Lucienne. No need to throw it away; this evening when I come home I'll give it to my wife.

I attempt to step back, to see the advantages of my position and look on Julien's happiness with magnanimity. I tell myself it's all for the best. To snatch away the life of a young woman, at my age, and do nothing of value for her, would be quite wicked. I tell myself this, but they're just empty words and my heart is not magnanimous. It's too soon for me to feel like that. Later, much later—in a few days, when Renée has taken me in hand again.

"Come on out," says Julien. "There's a real April sun out here. Let's go and live."

XV

UNCLE ANTONIN HAS CHOSEN a corner table with a view of the door, but he doesn't see us come in, concentrating instead on the cars he is sketching on the back of the menu. I say, "Hello Uncle." He shakes Julien's hand and mine, not noticing that my old face is back. He only realises when we're already seated and I'm facing him.

"But it's you!" he exclaims, stupefied. "What on earth are you doing here?"

He stares at me, aghast, his eyes full of questions and accusations. There follows a scene of farcical misunderstanding which amuses our fellow diners not a little, for Uncle will not keep his voice down. Seeing how nervous and irritated I am, Julien intervenes.

"Please calm yourself," he says to Uncle Antonin. "I think I understand from what you've said that you know of the existence of a certain Roland Colbert who has been trying to impersonate Raoul. I have told your nephew the whole story. Raoul himself knows the individual in question; he met him a number of times before his journey to Bucharest, and thinks him a lunatic but completely harmless. As for the metamorphosis, it's perfectly understandable that you believed his story. The creature is diabolically persuasive and he was very close to convincing me too, I can assure you. All in all, the best thing is to forget the whole affair, since it doesn't matter much in the end."

At these last few words, Uncle's expression, which had relaxed somewhat, begins to worry me again. His lip trembles and his long moustache follows suit. I fear an outburst. Indeed, he half-stands and cries out in a thunderous voice:

"Doesn't matter! Miserable man: that swine has dishonoured you, he has slept with your wife!"

Everyone's eyes are fixed on us. The manager glares coldly at our table.

"Uncle, please, don't make so much noise. And don't be so quick to accuse Renée. I know she went out at least once with this man, for Julien saw them. I also know that he had an apartment in our building. Does this really mean that your niece was having an affair? Frankly, I don't think so at all."

I'm afraid he'll make a fuss over my gullibility in an attempt to make truth and justice triumph, but I forestall him.

"You do understand, Uncle, that if I had the slightest reason to believe that Renée were cheating on me, it would mean immediate separation?"

He resolves to be silent, unhappily pulling on his moustache as if on a gag restraining him. Julien directs the conversation to other subjects, but he is practically the only speaker. Uncle is gloomy and I am too. To distract him from his melancholy I ask if his car has had any major transformations during my absence. My question seems to revive him a little. He tells us about a neat new invention that he's thinking of patenting. It's a kind of low-powered emergency engine, whose compact dimensions allow it to be stored underneath an ordinary car seat. He fires up with enthusiasm, as on his best days, when suddenly his thoughts turn to something else and he breaks off, sighing:

"Such a pity, all the same."

"What's a pity, Uncle?"

"I was thinking of that metamorphosis. One would so have liked it to be true."

He fell silent. I am touched by his regret, which is like that of a child giving up some fantasy.

"Are you honestly sorry about that?" asked Julien, who wanted to put his finger on the exact meaning of this statement. "But why?"

"It must be because I'm old," Uncle Antonin offered.

I protest, and Julien too, that he's not getting old and that he has actually proved his own youthfulness by believing in his nephew's metamorphosis. He shakes his head.

"No, no, you're mistaken. I believed in it because I am old. It's been a couple of days now since I started to wonder, and I've thought it through now. I am old."

"Normally," Julien observed, "old age is not very receptive to great changes."

"That's possible. But at my age, time passes quickly, very quickly, you'll see for yourselves in the end. And it's a strange sensation, which makes you want to shake yourself, a feeling of being caught up in a machine that never misfires, can never break down. It's exhausting, this mechanism that runs so well. One would like to see it go wrong just once in a while, even if nothing ultimately changes the order of things. It would be a respite, at least. We older people, when you see us going back to mass, you think it's just a precaution, but the truth is it's the machine that's bothering us and we'd like to send a note to the mechanic. I'm sure of it, I really am. On the days when I think God exists, I'm always trying to challenge him to make the machine go backwards. And then, well, one has to admit these things. I really liked this Roland Colbert fellow. Pleasant, good-looking, young, and he had such beautifully feminine eyes; I said to myself, basically, it's a fantastic chance for Raoul. And then, this idea of coming and telling you: 'Look, my face has changed, but really it's me, Raoul Cérusier'—it's not just anyone could have come up with that one."

Uncle looks long and critically at me, and adds, shaking his head:

"Of course, you would never have come up with a scam like that."

This time, entering the premises of the government office from which less than six weeks ago I left with a different face, I am apprehensive almost to the point of panic. On the landing, before I step through the doorway, I glance at myself in my small pocket mirror. It's still me. I enter. I can see Mme Passavent's grey hair behind the service window, as she hunches over her paperwork. On the public side, M Caracalla is chatting to the clerk in the next window. His silver-topped cane is hooked onto the wooden ledge, on which he's also leaning cosily on his elbows, one finger to his cheek. He gives me a brief side-ways glance and continues to speak, but more loudly:

"I made myself known and when they realised who I was, they apologised for everything."

I seek out the stocky shape of M Boussenac in the depths of the office, but already the light is bad. They are starting to turn on the lamps again.

"Here it is," said Mme Passavent, in a neutral tone. "Have you your papers?"

Without looking at me, she gathers up the pile of docu-ments I've stacked in front of her, sets aside the request on headed notepaper and opens a large, green, cloth-bound register.

"Do you have the photographs?"

I lay two photos on the counter, my heart beating loudly. The action is enough for Mme Passavent, who starts to write in her register without even a cursory look at the photos. I know this will take her some time. Idly, I allow myself to drift back to my day's tasks, of which the most pressing is to find a good secretary for Lucienne to train before the end of the month. I would like one over fifty, or with a crooked nose, though I'm also secretly hoping for a charming surprise. In all honesty, it hardly bothers me. Apart from a few minute differences, my life today is so similar to what it was two months ago, it's re-established its old ways with such assurance and solidity that the smile of a charming secretary will never distract me much again. Even if Lucienne's marriage were to break down and she were to fall in love with me again, it would already be too late. What a wife I have, and with what a good head and a warm heart too, however I might try to mock her in secret. Darling sweet Renée. The night of the bunch of violets, she was touched by my gesture and her pleasure shone so plainly in her face that our meal that evening was wholly amiable, and God seemed to be floating overhead. I managed to forget my separate bedroom and when it was time to retire, I returned to our bed naturally, scarcely apologetic, and magnanimous statements came easily to mind. The following night did, however, prompt me to act somewhat differently. Thanks to a bout of insomnia, I had a resurgence of pride that made me count my humiliations and rebel against their resumption. Shame and anger took over and made my head ache. With clammy skin and burning forehead, I tossed and turned, unable to find relief. Beside me Renée was sleeping peacefully, and suddenly her perfect sleep and regular breathing were like an insult, like the willed indifference of a cynic. I resolved to get up, to dress, and when she opened her eyes, to say: "I've an appointment at half-past twelve tonight." But I pictured myself wandering cold streets in search of an adventure I didn't really want. I stayed in bed. Tomorrow, I thought, I'll have my bed made up in the blue room again. Eventually, my anger dispersed into sleep. Since that night, I have gradually and smoothly readapted to a life of happiness and tranquillity. The memory of my metamorphosis does not disturb the harmony of our household. I never bring up the subject of Renée's unfaithfulness, for I see in it nothing more than a wayward notion that went too far. As for the rest, we're always conscious of it, Renée in particular.

At first, I flattered myself that my superior, knowledge-able position gave me an advantage over my wife, but I see now I was wrong about that. Not only does she not feel the slightest embarrassment in front of me, she even finds a certain distinction in it for herself; something of the glory of the traveller who has basked in other climates but resigns herself graciously to a sedentary life. This superiority is evident from her slightly haughty gentleness, and also in her attitude of distraction and nostalgia which allow her frequently to cut me short, to close discussions and to decide on every matter with an air of unintention-al, distracted authority which excuses her from debate. I do not cease to be amazed at her aplomb in recovering from a situation which would have embarrassed me a great deal in her place. And then, the other day, being somewhat annoyed, I decided to make her understand the generosity and goodwill behind my submission, when I could so easily have fallen back on contempt.

It was a Sunday morning. We were both in the bath-room, where I was busy shaving and Renée was linger-ing in a bath, taking no notice of me. She examined her naked, slender body slowly, privately, from the tips of her toes to those of her breasts, which, supported by the buoyant water, were looking rather fine. In a blank, distracted voice, as if she were thinking aloud, she broke the silence to declare:

"The Gémillards can think what they like, it's too bad; we shan't go round there this afternoon."

The Gémillards are old friends from my side of the family for whom I retain a sincere affection, and I enjoy seeing them for the memories of provincial life that we share. In order not to annoy Renée, who thinks them vulgar and tedious, I restrict myself to seeing them no more than twice or three times a year. We haven't seen them now for more than six months, and happening to run into old M Gémillard in the middle of the week, I have promised we'll visit on Sunday afternoon. My first move was to protest against Renée's decision. But I soon understood that my objections would have no effect. Renée would listen without complaint and, two or three hours later, would mention the business as if it were understood and agreed upon. "I'll call them and make our excuses," she would say. I reflected that to make her change her mind I would have to aim further than this minor question, but I had no desire to jeopardise our modus vivendi once more. Yet the seconds were passing and still I had said nothing. Glancing in the mirror, I caught a triumphant smile on Renée's face. I set down my razor and perched on the edge of the bath.

"You ought really to know the truth, all the same. I never went to Bucharest."

She looked at me, suddenly fearful, realising I was about to effect a great reversal that would threaten her peace of mind. Faced with the risk of a serious, even stormy argument, her nudity, which had just given her such satisfaction, troubled her suddenly, like a weakness. She tried to cover herself with her hands.

"The evening I announced that I was going to Bucharest, I had just had a very strange experience. That afternoon, I had gone to obtain a B O B licence and, at the counter, the clerk had refused to accept my identity photos, claiming that they looked nothing like me. Called on to give their opinions, the other staff agreed with her."

"But that's quite mad," exclaimed Renée, in exaggerated indignation, intended no doubt to flatter me in my narration.

"After a fairly long dispute, I leave. Then I meet Julien Gauthier on the Pont Royal and I go towards him thinking we'll shake hands. He looks at me like a stranger and declares he doesn't know me."

"Well!"

"Astounded, I rush to find a shop where I can see myself in the mirror and I don't recognise myself either."

While I was speaking, I saw that Renée was already reassured by the very extravagance of my story. I added in a low voice, shaking with emotion, like that of an actor in a melodrama—

"My face had changed!"

Renée smiled at this childish story, and said generously, in recognition of my attempt to amuse her:

"You are silly, darling."

I laughed my loud Cérusier laugh. I could have continued, could have told her how I had seduced her and given her disturbing details of our intimate moments. I would have worried her without convincing her, and besides I hadn't the will to delve into the twists of our adventure. Nevertheless, I wanted to make use of the moment to ask her a question that had been troubling me.

"My story is silly. But suppose my face had really changed. Suppose that, that evening, a stranger with bright, attractive eyes and the same voice as me, same clothes, same writing, and somehow knowing our most private secrets, had come and told you: 'I am your husband.' What would you have done?"

At any other time, Renée would have claimed that my question was nonsense, for she rarely has much taste for imaginative exercise. But she probably thought that in telling her this very dull little tale, whose trigger seemed to be the Gémillard incident, I had at first had some idea of attacking her, but had changed my mind in the middle and chosen another tack. Careful not to anger me, she replied with the care that she takes with everything and, after a moment's thought, replied:

"I would have thrown him out of the house."

"I'm not sure you would. You would have had to account for a whole range of coincidences which together would have amounted almost to proof of his story."

Renée thought again. I sensed that she was caught up in the game and that the elements of the problem had become quite real to her. I summed up her dilemma: "Accept a monstrous, absurd reality, or run the risk, the very great risk of cutting off your lifelong husband for ever." Her gaze hardened and an inward violence suffused her face. Out of a scruple of conscience, she was prolonging a private debate, but I guessed that she had already decided the outcome, perhaps without even knowing it herself. A profound and imperative instinct led her to prefer the human risk over that intrusion of the absurd which, it seemed to her, would distort, even extinguish all natural life.

"I would definitely have thrown him out," she repeated, with a kind of relief.

"And if the stranger had offered you rock-solid proof?"

Renée sat up in the bath in order to soap herself and replied without hesitation:

"From the second it ceases to present any choice, the question becomes nonsense."

The discussion ended there and I took up my razor again. Renée thought it wise not to make any further objections to our visit to the Gémillards. So that afternoon at about three o'clock, all four of us left the house in order to call on our good friends. They live near the Porte des Ternes. It's a pretty walk. At first I strolled between my wife and my little Toinette, who held my hand. Lucien walked a few steps ahead of us, looking glum and dragging his feet, for I have to concede he too had no great affection for the Gémillards. We were on Rue Caulaincourt, just at the highest point of the curve, and I was saying to Lucien, irritated, "Look, Lucien, walk in front or beside us, but don't be forever throwing yourself right in our way," when I saw the Sarrazine approaching, walking with a friend. They seemed to be having a serious and private discussion. The Sarrazine's beautiful masculine face was leaning thoughtfully towards that of her girlfriend as the pair walked arm-in-arm. In this unselfconscious pose, her bearing was still that of a pure-blood; an Arab mare, as testified by her finely shaped legs and proud shoulders. I looked at her again just as she passed us. She didn't see me. I know she will never see me again. Renée, who had missed nothing of the direction and intensity of my look, said untruthfully: "Did you see that enormous woman who just went past us? The boyish airs she was putting on? You can see straight away what kind *she* is." I didn't answer.

All the lamps are lit. M Caracalla shifts his cane along, so that it hangs on his right side, and as he does this, he allows his eyes to stray as far as me. He has seen my two identity photos lying on the counter, and this reminds him of something. "Talking of which," he says to the clerk, "have you seen any more of that crackpot who was so determined to show that he looked like someone else's photo?" The clerk made a gesture indicating she'd heard nothing more. I can see the rotund silhouette of M Boussenac, sitting in a circle of light at the far end of the office, engrossed in the pages of a huge ledger.

Mme Passavent has finished writing in her register. She picks up my photos and sets them on her desk. When the moment comes for her to stick them down, she glances at them briefly, just as she had that other time, and I feel the two occasions becoming one, and my adventure playing itself out in the space of one extended, monstrously dilated elastic second that eventually contracts into itself, so that in truth, it has been no more than a moment.

TRANSLATOR'S AFTERWORD

TOWARDS THE END of the last century, after his death in 1967, Marcel Aymé was commonly dismissed as a writer of light fiction. Perhaps because he became best known for his series of whimsical farmyard tales for children, *Les Contes du Chat Perché*. However, he wrote prolifically in many genres, including theatre, screenplays, novels and short stories, and in his heyday was highly regarded by his fellow writers in Paris. He corresponded with Camus and Gide, adapted a Maigret story for film, and translations of his novels were regularly reviewed as far afield as *Time* magazine (whose reviewer found him extraordinarily sceptical and pessimistic, and likened him to Buster Keaton). Today his short stories are recognised as among the best of twentieth-century short fiction, particularly admired for their introduction of the fantastic into everyday Parisian settings. Aymé's literary roots run deep, showing the influence of Kafka and the surrealists but also of that French tradition of scepticism and humanism that began with Rabelais and the eighteenth-century philosophers and satirists.

Is Marcel Aymé difficult? Yes and no—*Beautiful Image* is a novel with a simple premise, explored without digression or sub-plot; it has few characters, including a strong narrator who is the head of an ordinary household; it raises uneasy questions, but allows resolution with a happy ending. However, Aymé's original readers would have felt the tensions inherent in this wry, comical story of a stroke of enchantment in the heart of bourgeois Paris.

Aymé sets his tale specifically in the streets of Montmartre and the area between the Arc de Triomphe and the Stock Exchange. He obliges Raoul Cérusier, a narrow-minded businessman, to investigate the complex relationship between face and character. He lays out Cérusier's elations and miseries in the most straightforward way—but he would never presume simply to tell us the answer to his fundamental question: *Are* we what we look like? Instead, his narrative floats somewhere between Cérusier's stolid observations and hints of greater truths.

There is comedy to be enjoyed along the way—which is the hardest thing to render in another language. Aymé's trademark wordplays and neologisms are occasionally tricky to understand, generations later, never mind to translate. But the effort is repaid by an insight into a complex, creative mind and its era—doubly fascinating as it now lies on the border between history and our modern times.

There is just one word perhaps necessary to gloss: *Sarrazine*. In English she would of course be the Saracen. However, her essential mystery and femininity would both disappear in the translation, so I have left her name as a name, its other meanings only a small step further from the English reader than the French.

This translation would not have been possible if it hadn't been read over by some very good friends: Pauline Le Goff, Cécile Menon and my father Harold Lewis were wonderfully patient; Yann Chatreau helped me to answer pages of questions to myself over kirs in La Trouvaille; Michelle Thomas provided the expertise on Marcel Aymé which allowed me to crack the toughest of Ayméisms. Thank you.

SOPHIE LEWIS